Killer Cruise

**Center Point
Large Print**

**This Large Print Book carries the
Seal of Approval of N.A.V.H.**

A Jaine Austen Mystery

Killer Cruise

Laura Levine

CENTER POINT PUBLISHING
THORNDIKE, MAINE

F
L e v

This Center Point Large Print edition
is published in the year 2009 by arrangement with
Kensington Publishing Corp.

Copyright © 2009 by Laura Levine.

All rights reserved.

The text of this Large Print edition is unabridged.
In other aspects, this book may vary
from the original edition.
Printed in the United States of America.
Set in 16-point Times New Roman type.

ISBN: 978-1-60285-500-7

Library of Congress Cataloging-in-Publication Data

Levine, Laura, 1943-
  Killer cruise / Laura Levine. -- Center Point large print ed.
    p. cm. -- (A Jaine Austen mystery)
  ISBN 978-1-60285-500-7 (lib. bdg. : alk. paper)
  1. Austen, Jaine (Fictitious character)--Fiction.
    2. Women detectives--California--Los Angeles--Fiction.
    3. Murder--Investigation--Fiction. 4. Cruise ships--Fiction.
    5. Los Angeles (Calif.)--Fiction. 6. Large type books. I. Title. II. Series.

PS3612.E924K57 2009
813'.6--dc22

2009014825

Chapter 1

The good news about my cruise is, I didn't get seasick. The bad news is, I almost got hacked to death by a raving loony. But, hey. Life's funny that way. My life, that is. Just when I think things are going smoothly someone comes along and tries to eviscerate me.

But let's rewind to the day it all began, shall we?

My neighbor Lance was stretched out on my bed, watching me as I raced around tossing clothes into a suitcase.

"I still can't believe you're going on a cruise by yourself," he said, shaking his blond curls in disbelief.

Yes, it's true. I, Jaine Austen, a woman whose idea of a Mexican vacation is a two-for-one Burrito Day at Taco Bell, was about to head off on my first cruise to Mexico. Or, as we cognoscenti say, *Me-hi-co!* And the best thing was, it was absolutely free!

I'd answered an ad in the *L.A. Times* from a cruise company looking for lecturers, and much to my surprise and delight, they'd hired me. All I had to do was teach a few lessons on Writing Your Life Story, and the generous folks at Holiday Cruise Lines were picking up my tab.

"But, Jaine," Lance pointed out, "the average age on these cruises is dead. How do you expect to meet anybody?"

"I'm not going on the cruise to meet anybody. I'm going for the adventure, the scenery, the Latin culture."

Oh, who was I kidding? I was going for the twenty-four hour buffet. Imagine! Dessert on tap any time day or night. Talk about heaven.

"Gaack! You can't possibly be taking that," Lance said, pointing to a perfectly serviceable *Cuckoo for Cocoa Puffs* T-shirt. "They'll make you walk the plank in that thing."

"This happens to be a collector's item," I sniffed.

"A garbage collector's," he sniffed right back.

Some people just don't appreciate kitsch.

"I'm sorry I can't take you to the pier like I was supposed to," he said, grimacing at a pair of my elastic-waist shorts, "but I've got to be at work in a half hour."

"That's okay. It's not your fault I'm running so late," I said, eyeing my cat, Prozac, who was perched atop my dresser. "A certain someone took a tinkle on my open suitcase this morning. Which meant I had to run out and buy a new suitcase and do an emergency load of laundry, which slowed me down a good hour or three."

Prozac glared down at me through slitted eyes that seemed to say:

You're lucky it was just a tinkle.

"Poor thing is upset that you're going away," Lance tsked.

"Upset? That's putting it mildly. Think King

Kong with hairballs. I don't see why you're making such a fuss, Pro. After all, Grandma and Grandpa are flying in all the way from Florida to take care of you."

Her tail twitched the way it always does when she's on the warpath.

Your parents are not *my "grandma" and "grandpa." And if your mother tries to put a bow in my hair like she did the last time, I won't be held responsible for the consequences.*

"Hey, I'd better get going," Lance said, springing up from my bed, "or I'll be late for work. Which reminds me, we're having a sale on Jimmy Choo. Want me to pick up a pair for you?"

Lance, who is gainfully employed as a shoe salesman at Neiman Marcus, can never seem to remember that the only thing I can afford from Jimmy Choo is his box.

"No, thanks." I smiled wanly.

"Well, good-bye then," he said, taking me in his arms for a farewell hug. "Have fun on the poop deck, whatever the heck that is."

After Lance left to fondle rich ladies' feet at Neiman's, I finished packing, all the while dreaming of seven days lolling in a deck chair and soaking up the sun. When I was done, I turned to Prozac, who was still glaring at me from her perch atop my dresser.

"So long, sweetheart," I said, scooping her in my arms. "You be good now, hear?"

Yeah, right. Whatever.

Wriggling free from my grasp, she leapt onto my bedspread, which she began clawing with a vengeance. I'd be surprised if it was still in one piece when I got back.

I picked up my bags and headed out to the living room, fighting back waves of guilt. In spite of Prozac's abominable behavior, I felt bad about leaving her. What can I say? When it comes to my cat, I'm a hopeless sap, mere putty in her paws.

Oh, well. I couldn't fret. Prozac would be fine. My mother would stuff her with human tuna and spoil her rotten.

I took one last look around my apartment, bidding farewell to my overstuffed sofa and my straggly philodendron plant, then headed outside.

It was a glorious day, complete with crayon-blue skies, fluffy white clouds, and palm fronds rustling in the breeze. What perfect weather to set sail for the high seas. Luckily I'd nabbed a parking spot in front of my duplex. I loaded my suitcase and tote bag in the trunk of my car and was just about to shut the lid when I realized I'd forgotten to pack my *Giant Book of New York Times Crossword Puzzles*, which I intended to work my way through during my seven days at sea, a succession of free strawberry smoothies at my side.

With a sigh of impatience, I dashed back to my apartment and into my bedroom, where Prozac had abandoned my bedspread and was now busily attacking my pillow. I could've sworn I'd left the crossword book on my night table, but it wasn't there.

I looked in the living room, the bathroom, and kitchen, and was about to give up when I finally saw it peeking out from under the living room sofa. No doubt Prozac had hidden it there—just her thoughtful way of saying "bon voyage."

I grabbed it and raced back out to the Corolla, where I tossed it into the trunk and got behind the wheel, excitement mounting. At last I was headed off for a fabulous week of cruising!

Bidding adieu to the cares and woes of my workaday life, I took off with a smile on my lips and a song in my heart.

And—what I didn't know at the time—a cat in the trunk of my car.

Chapter 2

Prozac, the little devil, had undoubtedly slipped out of my apartment while I was dashing around looking for my crossword puzzle book. Like an idiot, I'd left the front door open.

Now as I opened the trunk of my car in the pier's parking lot, she sauntered out from where she'd been hiding behind my suitcase and looked up at me in triumph.

Anchors aweigh!

Oh, Lord. Fifteen minutes till final boarding.

There was no way I could possibly get her back to my apartment. And they'd never let me on board with a cat.

Of course, I could always come clean and confess all. But I wasn't about to give up my free cruise. Not to mention my chances of ever working for Holiday Cruise Lines again. Here was my golden opportunity to wow them with my lecture skills, and line up a whole roster of glam cruises around the Pacific. I'd already mentally booked a twenty-one-day excursion to Tahiti. I simply couldn't give all that up and spend the next seven days back in my apartment watching The Weather Channel with my parents.

No, there was only one sensible thing to do under the circumstances:

Smuggle Prozac on board.

"Okay, kiddo," I said, plopping her into my tote bag. "You're about to become a stowaway."

I zipped up the bag, leaving it open just enough so that she'd get some air.

"And if you don't want Grandma putting bows in your hair for the next week," I hissed as I made my way to the embarkation area, "then stay put and be quiet."

My palms were sweaty as I handed over my suitcase to a burly baggage handler. I prayed Prozac wouldn't blow it and start wailing from the tote. But Prozac had obviously gotten the message and was keeping her mouth shut.

Once my suitcase was loaded onto a dolly, I headed inside a cavernous barn of a building where passengers were chattering happily, waiting on line to get through security.

I quickly called Lance on my cell and left a message on his voice mail, telling him what happened and asking him to please tell my parents I had Prozac with me. Then I took my place at the end of the line, behind a couple with a toddler in a stroller.

All was going according to plan as we inched our way to the security scanner. Nary a peep from the tote bag. I was beginning to think I was going to get away with my stowaway scheme when the toddler in front of me shrieked:

"Kitty cat! Kitty cat!"

I looked down, and to my horror, I saw that Prozac had wriggled her head out of the tote and was looking around, surveying the scene. I promptly shoved her back down again.

"Mommy! Mommy! Kitty cat!"

The kid tugged at his mother's jeans, getting her attention. She turned around, a harried brunette with an armful of tour books.

"What is it, Devon?"

"Kitty cat!" he screeched at the top of his lungs, in case anybody didn't hear it the first seven times.

"A cat?" his mom asked, looking around. "Where?"

"Oh, that was Snuffles," I said, with a moronic giggle. "My stuffed animal. I never go anywhere

11

without Snuffles. It's a security thing. I'm working on it in therapy. My therapist says I'm making very good progress, especially with my new meds. . . ."

I tend to babble when I'm nervous.

"Now, Devon," the kid's mother murmured, wheeling the stroller as far away from me as possible, "don't bother the crazy lady."

Okay, so she didn't call me crazy, but I could tell she was thinking it.

By now we'd reached the security scanner.

Holding my breath, I put my tote bag on the conveyor belt.

I cringed as I saw it moving from within. I fully expected a zillion alarms would go off and I'd be arrested as a cat-smuggling terrorist. But thankfully, nobody else seemed to notice.

Now it was my turn to walk through the human scanner. I pasted a sickly smile on my face and stepped inside, my heart racing at Indy 500 speed, guilt oozing from every pore.

But the security guy just waved me through with a bored flap of his hand.

My heartbeat returned to normal as I retrieved my tote bag and headed outside. I was just about to cross the threshold to freedom when I felt someone clamp my arm in an iron grip.

"Just a minute, miss."

I whirled around to face another security guard, a beefy Brunhilde of a woman with biceps the size of volleyballs.

The jig was clearly up. Man overboard. Time to walk the plank.

"You forgot your crossword puzzles," she said, handing me my *Giant Book of New York Times Crossword Puzzles*.

I took it from her, my hands trembling with relief.

"Have a good trip," she said, with a big-toothed smile.

"Thanks so much," I managed to sputter.

Then I stepped outside to the dock, where I got my first glimpse of the *Holiday Festival*, a sparkling white behemoth of a ship trimmed with gleaming wood railings and lavish balconies.

Wow, I thought, gazing up at the beautiful vessel. This was the life!

Down below I could see workers loading crates of food supplies. I only hoped some of them contained chocolate.

I headed for the gangplank, where two ship's officers, handsome Scandinavians clad in white, wanted to see my passport. It was my one final hurdle, and I passed it with flying colors, if you don't count the nasty scratch Prozac gave me when I reached into my tote for my passport.

Operation Stowaway was a success!

At last, my carefree vacation at sea about to begin, I scooted up the gangplank.

Of course, if I'd known the hell that was in store for me, I would've scooted right back down again.

• • •

According to my ticket, my cabin was on the Dungeon Deck. Okay, technically, it was called the Paradise Deck, but it was so deep in the bowels of the ship, I practically got the bends riding down in the elevator.

But I didn't care. I was thrilled to have made it past security.

I was making my way along the corridor, looking for my cabin, when Prozac, clearly irritated at having been cooped up in a tote bag with nothing for company but my hair dryer, sprang out of the bag and began prancing down the corridor.

"Stop this instant!" I commanded in vain, bolting after her.

Then, just as I was about to catch her, a woman came out from her cabin, an attractive blonde with the statuesque good looks of a Vegas showgirl.

Of all the rotten timing.

"What do we have here?" she cooed, scooping Prozac up in her arms.

Instantly Prozac shot her one of her wide-eyed Adorable looks. Somehow, when it comes to strangers, Prozac always manages to turn on the charm.

"Oh, god," I started babbling, "she snuck out of my apartment when I was looking for my cross-word puzzles and it was too late to bring her back home so I had to hide her in my tote bag because I couldn't give up seven days in the sun with a twenty-four-hour buffet and it was all going so smoothly until I found her in the trunk of my car. The last thing I need on this cruise is Prozac."

"I don't know about that, honey. You might want to take one of those Prozacs. Sounds like you could use one."

"No, you don't understand. Prozac is my cat."

"What a sweetheart," she said, scratching the little monster behind her ears.

"You're not going to tell anyone about her, are you? They're sure to quarantine her in some horrible cage, and even though that's just what she deserves, I couldn't bear for that to happen."

"Don't worry, hon." She flashed me a friendly smile. "Your secret's safe with me."

"Thank you so much!"

"I'm Cookie Esposito. I sing with the band in the Sinatra Lounge."

"I'm Jaine Austen. No relation," I quickly added, to forestall the question I've been asked 8,756 times in my life. "I'm one of the ship's lecturers. I'm teaching a course in Writing Your Life Story."

"A writer! How wonderful! Welcome to the Paradise Deck, Jaine. This is where they put all the hired hands. C'mon, I'll walk you to your cabin."

"It's right here," I said, spotting my cabin number.

"Great! Right next to mine," she grinned. "We'll be neighbors!"

What a stroke of luck. At least I'd have one

neighbor who wouldn't get suspicious if she heard meowing in the middle of the night.

"If there's anything you need, just knock on my door. Bye, snookums."

This last endearment was addressed to Prozac, whom she reluctantly handed back to me and then headed off down the corridor.

I took the keyless entry pass card I'd been given and put it in the electronic door lock. A green light flashed, and I turned the handle.

Because I was traveling for free, I wasn't hoping for anything lavish in the way of accommodations. I'd kept my expectations low. But apparently not low enough. I blinked in dismay as I stepped into a windowless cubbyhole of a room with all the charm of a broom closet. There was barely room for me and my suitcase, which had been jammed between two narrow twin beds.

Prozac surveyed the scene.

For this I spent forty minutes in the trunk of your car?

With that she leaped up onto one of the beds and began sniffing around, no doubt hoping to uncover some minced mackerel on the bedspread.

Somehow I managed to jam my clothes into the cabin's microscopic closet, then locked my wallet in the room safe, thrilled that I wouldn't be needing it for the next seven days.

I was about to stretch out on one of the beds for a much deserved rest when I realized that there was only one pillow in the cabin—and Prozac was sprawled on it.

"Upsy daisy," I said, lifting her up. "Mommy needs to rest."

She shot me a laser look.

You're not my mommy and I want my pillow back.

I had no sooner rested my head on the pillow when I felt her land with a thud in the general vicinity of my left ear. The next thing I knew, her tail was in my mouth. I gave her a gentle push, and she gave me a not-so-gentle scratch. One thing led to another and we were in the middle of a most undignified scuffle when I heard a knock on the door.

"Who is it?" I called out.

A soft unintelligible reply came from out in the corridor.

I quickly stashed Prozac in the glorified wash-basin posing as my bathroom and poked my head out the door.

A skinny guy of indeterminate nationality, dressed in what looked like a bellhop's uniform, stood in the corridor.

"I'm Samoa," he said. "Your steward."

At least I think his name was Samoa. His accent was so thick I couldn't be sure.

"Samoa show you around your cabin."

Not much of a trip there. Besides, I doubted there'd be room for both of us.

17

"No need," I said. "I'm fine."

"You sure?"

His big brown eyes peered over my shoulder into the cabin. In the background I thought I heard Prozac meowing, but thankfully, Samoa didn't seem to notice.

"I'm fine," I assured him. "Just wonderful."

"You need anything, just call Samoa."

What I needed was another pillow, but I couldn't risk having him come back to the cabin.

"Right. Great. Thanks so much," I said, shutting the door on his smiling face.

I clamped my ear to the door until I heard his footsteps fading down the hallway. Then I let Prozac out of the bathroom and sank down into the cabin's one and only chair. Obviously I was going to have to keep my DO NOT DISTURB sign on my door the entire trip.

"Thanks to you, Pro, I'll be making my own bed for the next seven days."

I'd have to call housekeeping and cancel steward service. Maybe I'd tell them that I was allergic to cleaning products, and that I couldn't have anyone in my room who'd even touched a can of cleanser or I'd break out in hives. That might work.

I was just about to reach for the phone when I heard another knock on the door.

Drat. Not again.

"Who is it?"

"It's me. Cookie."

I opened the door and found her standing there holding a large plastic bin filled with sand.

"A present for Prozac," she grinned. "A litter box."

A litter box! I'd forgotten all about that.

"C'mon in," I said, ushering her inside. Cookie was clearly shaping up to be my shipboard guardian angel. "Where on earth did you get it?"

"I filched the tray from the busboys' station at the buffet and the sand from the kiddie sandbox."

"What do you think, Pro?" I said, putting the makeshift litter box down in the bathroom.

She walked over and sniffed at it, clearly unimpressed.

What? No Mountain-Fresh Pine scent?

"I'm afraid she doesn't like it," Cookie sighed.

"She'll learn to like it," I said, glaring at Prozac. "Meanwhile, how can I ever thank you? You've been such an angel."

Just as she was assuring me that no thanks were necessary, the captain's voice came over the public-address system announcing the ship's safety drill.

"C'mon," Cookie said, grabbing two life vests from my closet. "We'll go together."

Leaving Prozac lolling on the fought-after pillow, I headed out for my first official event of the cruise.

"First we have to pick up Graham," Cookie said when we were out in the corridor.

"Graham?"

"Graham Palmer III." Her eyes lit up. "He's my boyfriend. Wait'll you meet him. He's a real dreamboat.

"Graham, sweetie," she called out, knocking on one of the cabin doors. "It's me."

Cookie did not lie. Graham Palmer III was a dreamboat of the highest order. He came to the door in white slacks and blue blazer—tall, tan, and graying at the temples. In a former life, he may well have been Cary Grant.

"Hello, darling," he said, in a British accent that reeked of high tea in the Cotswolds.

"And who might this be?" he asked, flashing me a dazzling smile.

"This is Jaine," Cookie announced. "She's a writer. And one of the ship's lecturers."

"Welcome to paradise, Jaine."

Another dazzling smile, this one accompanied by a wink. The guy was a charmer, all right.

"Graham's one of the ship's Gentlemen Escorts. You know, the men they hire to dance with the single ladies."

"But my heart belongs to Cookie," Graham said, kissing her lightly on the lips.

"It's true," Cookie beamed. "Graham's heart really does belong to me. See for yourself."

She lifted a pendant from her generous cleavage and held it out for me to inspect.

It was a gold half-a-heart, engraved with her initials, with a jagged line where the heart had been divided in two.

"Graham's got the other half. Go on, Gray. Show it to her."

He pulled out a matching half-a-heart from under his blue-and-white-striped sport shirt. Like Cookie's, his pendant had been personalized with his initials, engraved in a fussy curlicued script.

"See? They fit," Cookie said, putting them together. "It's a symbol of our commitment to each other. Isn't that sweet?"

"Very." Any sweeter, I'd need a diabetes shot.

"C'mon, darling," Graham said. "We'd better get a move on."

Because elevator use was forbidden in the safety drill, we had to clomp up about a zillion stairs to where our passenger group was meeting in the Tiki Lounge. If this was what I'd have to endure in an emergency, I'd opt for going down with the ship.

The Tiki Lounge was done up in an ersatz Hawaiian motif—complete with fake palm trees, tiki masks on the walls, and a thatched canopy over the massive bar.

We put on our unflattering life vests and listened as one of the ship's officers, standing under a stuffed marlin, lectured us about emergency evacuation procedures. Thank heavens they let us sit in the lounge's booths while the officer droned on. I was sitting there watching Cookie and Graham play kneesies under the table when I became aware of a strange-looking guy at the next booth giving me the eye.

You should know that about me. Somehow I always seem to attract life's weirdos. This one had a long, greasy ponytail and an unbelievably bad Sunkist Orange bottled tan.

Quickly averting my gaze, I went back to watching the kneesies action.

At last the lecture was over, and we started to go. I hadn't taken three steps when I was cornered by Mr. Ponytail.

Up close I could see he had a stud in one of his nostrils.

"Allow me to introduce myself," he said, with an oily smile. "I'm Anton Devereux, Professional Ice Sculptor."

"Nice to meet you," I said, wondering if the stud hurt when he blew his nose.

"Of course, ice isn't the only medium where I ply my artistry."

Ply his artistry? It looked like somebody was a bit full of himself.

"I do it all—clay, granite, sand, and sometimes when finances are tight, chopped liver at bar mitzvahs."

"How interesting," I lied.

"You must come to one of my poolside demonstrations. In fact, perhaps you'd care to take a stroll on deck right now. I can tell you about the time I carved Venus de Milo out of tuna salad."

"Sounds like fun, but I've really got to go back to my cabin to finish unpacking."

And before he could say another word about his tuna fish Venus, I was out of there.

Needless to say, I'd lied to Mr. Ponytail. I did not go back to my cabin. Instead, I made my initial pilgrimage to the holy grail of cruising, the twenty-four-hour buffet. What with climbing all those stairs, I was feeling a bit peckish.

I already knew what deck the buffet was on. It was one of the first things I memorized when I got my cruise information packet in the mail. I was trotting down the hallway, wondering if they had hot fudge sundaes on tap, when I heard someone call my name.

I turned to see Paige McAllister, the ship's social director, heading in my direction.

I'd met Paige when I first came to the Holiday offices for my interview. A preppy blonde with shoulder-length hair swept back in a headband, she hadn't seemed all that impressed with my resume.

"You write toilet bowl ads for a living?" she'd asked, her perfectly plucked brows arched in disbelief.

"Toiletmasters happens to be one of the leading suppliers of plumbing fixtures in the greater Los Angeles area," I'd replied with as much dignity as I could muster.

"Is that so?" she'd said, with a dubious smile.

Frankly I'd been surprised when she'd called to offer me the gig.

She advanced on me now, clutching a clipboard.

"Welcome aboard, Jaine!" she chirped. "So glad you could join us. Just wanted to let you know you'll be meeting with your class in the Galley Grill Restaurant."

"We meet in a restaurant?"

"Yes, we often use our restaurants as lecture halls in the day to accommodate the crowds. Now remember. Our passengers are looking to be entertained. So keep it lively. Up and bubbly, that's our motto!"

"You bet!" I said, trying to put some bubble in my voice.

"And one more thing. I've got your dinner seating assignment."

"But I didn't request assigned seating."

"It's part of the job, Jaine. Many of our passengers like to be seated with the ship's celebrities. I've put you with the Pritchard party in the Continental Dining Room. The maitre d' will know where to seat you."

As flattered as I was to be thought of as a "celebrity," this whole dinner thing was a bit of a curveball. I hadn't expected to be eating with other people watching me. I guess that meant no doubles on desserts.

"And don't forget," Paige was saying,

"tomorrow night is Formal Night. You do have something appropriate to wear, don't you?"

Not unless she considered elastic-waist jeans and a *Cuckoo for Cocoa Puffs* T-shirt appropriate.

"Not exactly," I murmured, sans bubble.

True, I'd packed a pair of slacks and a few blouses for my classes, but I had nothing remotely formal. At the time I figured I'd be eating most of my meals at the casual buffet.

"No problem," she said, with an airy wave of her hand. "You can rent an outfit in the ship's rental shop. It shouldn't run you more than a hundred dollars or so."

A hundred bucks? It looked like the cruise wasn't going to be free after all. Oh, well. It was a small price to pay for seven heavenly days at sea.

After I assured Paige that I'd show up on Formal Night dressed to the nines, she told me with an insincere smile how marvy it was to have me on the Holiday team and then trotted off, clipboard akimbo.

Free at last, I took the elevator to the Baja Deck, home of the twenty-four-hour buffet. The room itself looked like an upscale cafeteria, with the buffet in the center, and tables on both sides looking out picture windows onto the open seas.

I gawked, openmouthed, at the vast cornucopia of chow on display: fresh-from-the-oven rolls, panini sandwiches grilled to perfection, rosy shrimp nestling in a bed of ice, barbequed chickens, honey-glazed ham, roast beef, and broiled salmon. Not to mention a mammoth salad bar and an overflowing fresh fruit basket.

And there—in the dessert section next to the apple pie, cherry cobbler, and chocolate éclairs— there in all their glory were fresh-from-the-oven brownies.

No doubt about it. I'd died and gone to calorie heaven.

I grabbed some shrimp for Prozac's dinner, and then, in a moment of restraint that was sure to go down in the next *Guinness World Records,* I took only one brownie for myself. This cruise was clearly going to be a floating snackfest of Olympic proportions, and I'd have to pace myself if I wanted to survive without busting my buttons.

Back in the cabin, Prozac and I scarfed down our chow eagerly. (I am happy to report my brownie was divine: moist and chocolatey, studded with nuts, and covered with a thick layer of frosting.)

When Prozac had finished inhaling her shrimp, she curled up on the fought-after pillow.

Wake me when it's time for the midnight buffet.

I rinsed out the bowl her shrimp had been in and filled it with water.

"Here's some water, Pro."

She eyed it balefully.

What? No champagne?

"It'll be in the bathroom, your majesty."

Leaving her purring like a buzz saw, I headed up

to the pool deck, where, according to my copy of the ship's newsletter, *Holiday Happenings*, the Set Sail Party was scheduled to take place.

It was already in progress when I showed up, a gala affair, complete with free leis and strolling mariachis.

As if on the Holiday payroll, the sun was in the midst of a spectacular sunset, sinking into the horizon in a blaze of glory.

I gazed out at the mass of gray heads surrounding me. True, there were a few honeymooners and couples with kids, but as Lance predicted, most of my fellow passengers were dedicated AARPsters.

But what did it matter if I was the only single woman on board with functioning ovaries? Not for me the shallow pursuit of romance. No, sir. I had my priorities straight.

I was content watching the sunset, smelling the sea, and eating my brownie.

(Okay, so I stopped off for another one.)

Chapter 3

Somehow I managed to cobble together a decent outfit for dinner that night: black slacks and a buttercream silk blouse I'd bought on sale at Nordstrom, topped off with a pair of simple pearls. I was going for an air of chic sophistication befitting my "celebrity" status.

"How do I look, Pro?" I asked, pirouetting in the few feet of space between our twin cots.

She peered up at me from where she was still encamped on the cabin's only pillow. I'd long since given up hope of ever resting my head on that thing again.

"So what do you think?"

She yawned a cavernous yawn.

I think I'd like a tuna melt.

Ignoring Prozac's pointed lack of interest in my outfit, I gave myself a final spritz of perfume and set out for the Continental Dining Room, eagerly awaiting my first free meal on board ship.

When I checked the menu posted outside the restaurant, my eyes zeroed in on one entrée: the "succulent filet mignon grilled to perfection, served with buttery mashed potatoes and creamed spinach."

No doubt about it. That was the dish for me.

Inside the restaurant, I was greeted by an unctuous maitre d' in a shiny white dinner jacket straight from the wardrobe department of *Casablanca.*

"*Bonsoir, mademoiselle,*" he crooned, in a thick French accent.

The oily smile that had been plastered on his face disappeared, however, when he checked my name on his seating chart.

"Austen, huh?" he said, his accent suddenly gone bye-bye. "You're being comped, right?"

"Yes, you see I'm giving a series of lectures on—"

"Whatever. Just don't order the filet mignon."

"Was he kidding? My salivary glands went into shock.

"We save the steaks for *paying* passengers."

Accent on "paying."

Grabbing a menu, he led me into a cavernous banquet hall of a room echoing with the excited buzz of people who hadn't yet been disappointed by their vacations.

As I weaved my way among the tables, I caught a glimpse of a happy passenger digging into his steak. Damn, it looked good. Charred on the outside, pink on the inside. Just the way I liked it. I felt like swooping down and snatching the fork out of his hand, but I figured that wouldn't exactly fit the image of a "celebrity" guest.

The maitre d' deposited me at a round window table where the Pritchard party, my assigned dinner companions, were already seated. One of them, I was surprised to see, was a tan, lanky guy in my age bracket.

"Mademoiselle Austen," the phony Frenchman announced with a flourish, his accent back in action.

Sad to say, I didn't get the celebrity greeting I'd been hoping for.

A sour dame with thin, grim lips and horn-rimmed glasses frowned at the sight of me.

"You're not Professor Gustav Heinmann, the Arctic explorer."

"No, I'm Jaine Austen, the writer."

"You can't be Jane Austen," she huffed. "She's been dead for centuries."

"That's Jaine with an *i*," I explained. "J-a-i-n-e."

"I don't care how it's spelled. I specifically requested to have Professor Heinmann at our table."

At which point, a sweet-looking old gal sitting next to her piped up.

"Now, Leona," she said. "I'm sure we're all thrilled to have a real writer at our table. Come, Ms. Austen, won't you have a seat?"

She patted the empty chair next to her, and I sat down, relieved I wasn't stuck next to the horn-rimmed gargoyle.

"I'm Emily Pritchard," she smiled. With her Wedgwood blue eyes and headful of soft gray curls, she looked like she'd just stepped out of a Norman Rockwell painting.

"Let me introduce you to everyone. First, my nephew Kyle."

A slick forty-something guy in designer togs nodded curtly.

"And this," Emily said, pointing to a faded blonde at Mr. Slick's side, "is Kyle's darling wife, Maggie." The blonde—who, like me, was packing a few extra pounds under her pantyhose—shot me a shy smile.

"And this is my other nephew, my adorable Robbie." Emily nodded at the lanky guy with the tan.

He was adorable, all right, with startling green eyes and a most appealing lopsided grin. I felt myself blush as he waved hello.

"And finally," Emily said, gesturing to Miss Congeniality in the horn-rimmed glasses, "my companion, Leona Nesbitt."

The sour dame barely managed a grunt.

"Every year I take my little family on a cruise," Emily gushed. "I adore cruising, always have ever since Daddy took me on my first voyage when I was eighteen years old."

"And we all appreciate your generosity, Aunt Emily." Kyle smiled, exposing small, sharklike teeth.

"But enough about us, Ms. Austen," Emily said. "Now you must tell us all about yourself and the wonderful books you've written."

Before I had a chance to tell her that the only book I'd ever written was *You and Your Garbage Disposal* for Toiletmasters Plumbers, the waiter came to take our order.

"And what will madame have?" he asked, starting with Emily.

"I'll have the steak. It looks simply divine."

Did it ever, I thought, still drooling over the hunk of red meat I'd seen on my way in.

"Do you think that's wise, dear?" Ms. Nesbitt

piped up. "You know how steak disagrees with you. Let's get the chicken, shall we?"

She shot the old lady a steely smile, and I could tell it wasn't so much a suggestion as a command.

"But surely, just this once . . ." Emily entreated.

"I don't think so, dear," her companion said firmly.

"I suppose you're right." Emily sighed in resignation. "I'll have the chicken."

Under no restrictions from the eagle-eyed Ms. Nesbitt, Kyle and Robbie both ordered the steak.

"Rare but not too rare," Kyle instructed the waiter, "or I'll send it back."

"Certainly, sir." The waiter nodded.

Ten to one, he'd be spitting in Kyle's food before the cruise was over.

"Oh, dear," Maggie said when it was her turn. "I can't seem to decide. The steak looks wonderful, but then, so does the halibut. And yet, you can never go wrong with chicken."

"Oh, for crying out loud, Maggie," Kyle snapped at his wife. "Make up your mind. You're keeping everyone waiting."

Maggie blushed and ordered the steak.

"And you, miss?" the waiter asked, turning to me.

I looked down at the menu, my eyes lingering on the filet mignon. Never had I wanted a steak so badly. Aw, what the heck? I'd order it. There was no way the maitre d' could find out. Not with this huge dining room full of passengers.

"I'll have the filet mignon," I said in a burst of defiance.

"Are you certain, madame?" The waiter shot me a warning look.

Oh, phooey. Clearly he'd been clued in on my second-class citizenship. If I ordered the steak, he was sure to rat on me to the maitre d'.

"On second thought," I sighed, "I'll have the chicken."

"Now Ms. Austen," Emily said, as our waiter trotted off with our orders, "you really must tell us all about your exciting life as a writer."

What on earth was I going to talk about? My ad campaign for Big John, the extra-large commode for extra-large people? Or my award-losing slogan for Ackerman's Awnings (*Just a Shade Better*)?

"I'm afraid it's not all that exciting."

"I'm sure it must be!" Emily beamed me an encouraging smile. "We want to hear all about your books."

"I haven't exactly written any books. I write advertising mainly."

"How marvelous!" Emily gushed. "Did you write *Got Milk?* I just love that!"

"No, I'm afraid not."

"So what *have* you written?" Nesbitt challenged.

"My clients are mostly local Los Angeles businesses. You've probably never heard of them."

"Go ahead," Nesbitt said, fixing me in her steely glare. "Tell us anyway."

She wasn't about to let this go. She liked seeing me squirm.

But I'd be damned if I'd let her intimidate me. So what if my credits weren't all that impressive? What could they do to me? Banish me to the buffet?

I squared my shoulders and began reeling off the names of my clients: "Toiletmasters Plumbers, Ackerman's Awnings, Fiedler on the Roof Roofers—

"Good heavens!" Emily exclaimed. "You wrote *Fiddler on the Roof*? Why that's one of my favorite musicals!"

"No, you don't understand—"

"We saw that on a theater cruise to London!"

And before I could straighten her out she was off and running about her cruise to London. It was pretty much that way throughout dinner, Emily rattling on, lost in memories of past cruises. I never did get to talk much about my life as a struggling writer of toilet bowl ads, and for that I was grateful.

When my chicken showed up, it was tasty enough, but I couldn't help but gaze longingly at the filet mignons around me.

Every once in a while Emily's stories were interrupted by Kyle snapping at his wife. (*Must you eat so fast? Do you really need another helping of those potatoes? For God's sake, Maggie, you've spilled gravy on your blouse.*) By the time dinner was over, I was ready to bop him with my butter knife.

Maggie ate her meal, eyes downward, absorbing his barbs, saying nothing. Across from her, Ms. Nesbitt polished off a disgustingly healthy vegetable plate, pausing only to shoot me a fish-eyed glare when I asked her to pass the rolls.

But most disconcerting was Adorable Robbie. Every time I glanced over at him, I saw him eyeing me appraisingly, grinning that lopsided grin of his.

Honestly, I was so discombobulated, I almost ordered the fruit cup for dessert.

Finally, the meal was over. Believe it or not, I hadn't eaten much. I'd felt awkward digging into my chow with my usual gusto, not with Robbie watching me like I was a contestant on *The Bachelor*.

"It's been lovely meeting you," I said to the others when we got up to go.

I was about to take off for the buffet to make up for lost calories when Robbie asked, "How about joining us in the lounge for an after-dinner drink?"

Whoa! Was this cutie actually interested in me? Or had he only asked me along because I was one of the few women on board not yet in menopause?

Whatever the reason, no way was I getting involved with him. After thirtysomething years on this planet, if I've learned one thing it's this: *The cute ones are dangerous*. Sooner or later, they're bound to make you miserable. And not only was this guy cute, he was Bad Boy cute. And they're the most dangerous of all.

Yes, red flags were waving. Klaxons were sounding. It was time to make my excuses and head for the buffet. For once in my life I'd do the smart thing and play it safe.

The words that actually came out of my mouth, however, were:

"Sure. I'd love to go."

What can I say? As my thighs would be the first to tell you, I'm seriously deficient in the willpower gene.

We all trooped over to the Sinatra Lounge, a dimly lit mahogany-and-leather affair, where Cookie, decked out in a spangly floor-length evening gown, was singing with a three-piece combo. Meanwhile, out on the dance floor, a few gray-haired couples were showing off their Arthur Murray dance moves.

The six of us grabbed seats near the action and gave our drink orders to a red-vested waiter. Emily, under the watchful eye of Ms. Nesbitt, ordered a Shirley Temple, as did the battle-axe herself. The rest of us opted for a wee drop of alcohol.

"I love listening to the old standards," Emily said when the waiter left, her feet tapping in time to the music. "They just don't write songs like they used to. Remember the time we met Johnny Mathis on our Caribbean cruise? Such a nice man! I still have his autograph on a cocktail napkin. I'll never forget what he wrote. *To Emily. Best wishes, Johnny Mathis.* Isn't that just the sweetest thing?"

"A real Pulitzer Prize winner," Kyle muttered under his breath.

"And Jaine, you'll never guess who we met on our cruise through the Panama Canal."

But I didn't get to hear who they met, because just then Cookie's boyfriend, Graham, glided up to our table.

"May I have the honor of this dance?" he asked Emily, in his velvety British accent.

No wonder the cruise line hired him. He cut quite the dashing figure in his blue blazer and perfectly creased slacks.

Emily looked up and flushed with pleasure.

But before she could reply, Nesbitt butted in.

"I don't think so, dear," she said, with a stern shake of her head. "Best let your dinner settle first."

"Oh, go ahead Aunt Emily," Robbie grinned. "Have some fun."

Emily hesitated a beat, looking first at Nesbitt and then at the handsome Gentleman Escort. Then Graham shot her one of his dazzler smiles, and the deal was sealed.

"I believe I would like to dance," she said, taking Graham's hand and beaming as he led her onto the dance floor.

"Honestly, Robbie," Nesbitt huffed, bristling

with annoyance. "Your aunt shouldn't be dancing so soon after dinner. It's bad for her digestion. You know what a weak stomach she has."

"Her stomach's fine, Leona. You're turning her into an old lady before her time."

"I think it's very sweet," Maggie piped up as Graham led Emily in a courtly fox-trot.

Kyle groaned in exasperation.

"Don't be ridiculous, Maggie. It's not sweet. It's obscene. The man is young enough to be her son."

"It's just a dance, Kyle," Robbie said. "Lighten up. Oh, wait, I forgot. You're constitutionally incapable of that."

Then he turned to me and, gesturing to the dance floor, asked, "Shall we?"

Once more, I warned myself not to get involved, and once more I caved like the marshmallow I am.

Out on the dance floor, Cookie was belting out "Just in Time," smiling indulgently as Graham twirled Emily around. She winked when she saw me with Robbie.

My temperature scooched up a few notches as he took me in his arms. Up close he was even cuter than he'd been across the dinner table. And he smelled like baby powder. I don't know about you, but I'm a sucker for a guy who smells like baby powder.

"I'm a big fan of your work," he said, his bad-boy grin back in action.

"What do you mean?"

"*In a Rush to Flush? Call Toiletmasters!* I've seen it on bus stops all over town. I'm assuming you wrote that."

"Guilty as charged."

"No, really. It's very catchy."

"If you've seen my ad, you must live in Los Angeles."

"In Santa Monica," he nodded. "The others live out in Pasadena. I'm the rebel of the clan."

"I'll bet you are."

"I never joined the family brokerage firm like Kyle. Instead, I moved out to the beach and got a job as a lifeguard. Now I make surfboards for a living."

Not exactly a captain of industry, but who cared? I'd long since given up trying to resist him. We finished that dance and started another. And another. I was floating around on a dreamy cloud, awash in a puddle of melted resolutions, when I felt someone tap me on the shoulder.

I turned to see who it was and my heart sank.

Oh, crud. It was Anton, the ice sculptor, decked out in Bermuda shorts and a loud Hawaiian shirt, his ponytail specially greased for the occasion.

"May I steal this lovely young lady for a dance?" he asked Robbie.

Say no, say no, say no, say no! I pleaded silently. But my prayers went unanswered.

I gulped in dismay as Robbie shot me a rueful

smile and turned me over to Anton, who instantly clutched me in a death grip and dragged me around the dance floor, mauling my toes with his two left feet, yakking about some swans he'd carved out of kielbasa sausage for a Polish wedding.

I counted the seconds till the song was over. But then, to my horror, I realized it was just the first in a medley of tunes, one song leading to another. And so I was trapped with Anton and his two lethal feet through a fox-trot, a mambo, and—horror of horrors—a jitterbug.

At last the music stopped and the nightmare came to an end.

"That was fun, wasn't it?" Anton asked in all seriousness.

"Yes, very." Like childbirth with a crowbar.

I couldn't wait to get back to where I'd left off with Robbie. But when I looked around the room, there was no sign of him.

So much for shipboard romance.

"So," Anton asked, "how about a moonlight stroll on deck?"

Not if he were the last ponytailed, sausage-sculpting bad dancer on earth—which he may well have been.

"Thanks, Anton, but I'm exhausted. I think I'm going to turn in."

And before he could stop me, I scooted to the exit. The last thing I saw as I headed out to freedom was Emily Pritchard out on the dance floor, still tripping the light fantastic with Graham.

It looked like dancing was good for her digestion after all.

I wasn't lying when I told Anton I was exhausted. After all the tumult of my first day at sea, I was in serious need of a tranquilizer or three. When the heck was the relaxing part of this vacation going to kick in?

I hurried along the corridor, checking over my shoulder to make sure Anton wasn't following me. Then, with the unerring accuracy of a homing pigeon, I returned to the buffet, where I picked up some roast beef for Prozac and a restorative dose of brownies for me.

It was too bad about Robbie ditching me, I thought, as I stowed my booty in some napkins. He probably saw a better-looking pair of functioning ovaries and decided to make a play for them. What did I tell you about the cute ones? Trouble with a capital *T.*

Banishing all thoughts of the beach bum with the bad-boy grin, I took the elevator down to my cabin in the Dungeon Deck.

I was feeling a bit guilty about leaving Prozac alone for so long, stuck in that tiny closet of a room. But it was her own fault, I reminded myself. Nobody asked her to sneak into the trunk of my car.

As it turned out, I needn't have worried about Prozac being lonely. Because when I opened the door to my cabin, I saw she had company.

There, sitting in the cabin's only chair with Prozac on his lap, was my steward Samoa.

"Good evening, Ms. Austen," he said, with a sly smile.

After recovering from what I'm certain was a mild coronary, I managed to squeak, "What are you doing here?"

"Samoa came to turn down bed."

Oh, rats. I'd forgotten to call housekeeping and cancel my maid service.

"Such a pretty kitty," he said, stroking Prozac.

I only hoped he didn't come from a country where she was considered an entrée.

"Such a pity," he said, "if kitty winds up in quarantine."

"Please don't tell anyone," I begged, then launched into a fevered explanation of Prozac's adventures as a stowaway.

"So you see," I concluded at the end of my recitation, "I didn't really mean to bring her on board."

Alas, he was unmoved by my tale of woe.

"Kitty not allowed on board ship," he said, his brown eyes cold as a calculator.

Damn. It looked like the little stoolie was going to turn her in.

"But Samoa won't tell."

"You won't?"

A ray of hope began to shine in my heart.

"On one condition," he added, that sly smile back in action.

I certainly hope he didn't expect any dipsy doodle. I love my cat, but there are limits, you know.

But he was not about to ask for sexual favors.

"You famous writer, right?"

"I'm not actually famous," I demurred, "although I am the proud recipient of the Los Angeles Plumbers Association's *Golden Plunger Award*."

He nodded, impressed. Which, I have to confess, is a reaction I don't get very often.

"You fix Samoa's book."

He looked down at the floor, and for the first time I noticed a huge pile of paper at his feet.

Dumping Prozac from his lap, he reached down and handed me what turned out to be nine hundred manuscript pages. All handwritten in a micro-scopic scrawl.

Oh, lord. He wanted me to edit his manuscript.

"Do not disturb," he intoned with great solem-nity.

Huh? Did he want me to edit his book or not?

Then I realized that was the title of his book: *Do Not Disturb* (spelled *Do Not Distub*).

He then proceeded to give me the highlights of the plot, a stirring opus of a swashbuckling steward who (in between changing bed linens) manages to foil an international terrorist plot on the high seas.

"Best seller," he nodded proudly.

Oh, yeah? In what universe?

"But Samoa's English not so good."

Tell me something I didn't already know.

"You fix for me."

I eyed the massive pile of handwritten pages. Yikes. This stuff made the Rosetta stone look like *Fun with Dick and Jane.*

"You fix by end of cruise."

"You've got to be kidding."

Sad to say, he was quite serious.

"You fix by end of cruise, or kitty goes to jail."

"Okay, okay," I sighed, kissing my relaxing vacation bye-bye.

YOU'VE GOT MAIL

To: Jaineausten
From: Shoptillyoudrop
Subject: What a Day!

Jaine, honey, what a day it's been. All I can say is, I refuse to fly with your father ever again. He spent the entire trip following the flight on his TV screen, convinced the captain was going the wrong way. Talk about your backseat pilots. He kept shouting things like, "Turn left at Amarillo! Left, dummy! Left!" Finally, the flight attendant asked him to lower his voice; said he was disturbing rows 14–27. Honestly, sweetheart, I was counting the seconds till we landed.

And then, when we got to your apartment, we got the fright of our lives. The key was just where you left it under the flowerpot, but your darling cat, Zoloft, was nowhere to be found!

Daddy was convinced somebody had broken into your apartment and stolen her. Which was ridiculous, of course, since all the windows were locked.

I thought maybe she was hiding. Or that she'd squeezed out through your mail slot and was roaming the city, lost and afraid. Cats have been known to squeeze through extremely small places. Why, just the other day on *America's Funniest Home Videos* I saw a cat who squeezed through a downspout. True, the cat got stuck in the downspout, which is why they sent in the video in the first place. But the point is, I was certain no one had broken into your apartment.

But you know how Daddy is. The next thing I knew he was calling the police and reporting a burglary!

Two of the nicest officers came by. Of course they said what I said all along, that there was no sign of forced entry. And even though they tried to hide it, I could tell they were peeved at Daddy for wasting their time.

Then just as they were driving away, your neighbor Lance showed up and told us that Zoloft was with you on the cruise. I had no idea you were allowed to bring pets on a cruise. Why didn't you tell us you were taking her, darling?

Lance was so sweet. He could see how upset we were, so he had us over to his apartment for cocoa and biscotti. He didn't even mind when Daddy lit up his smelly old pipe.

Did I tell you Daddy has started smoking a pipe? He bought it at a flea market last week and has been stinking up our condo ever since. I mean, who on earth smokes a *used* pipe?

He swears that it's a collector's item, that it was once smoked by Basil Rathbone in a Sherlock Holmes movie. Hah! The only thing it's collected is a bunch of old germs.

But Lance didn't seem to mind a bit. He's been so nice about everything, I've invited him to join us for dinner Tuesday night.

That's it for now, honey. Time to unpack.

Love and kisses,

Mom

To: Jaineausten
From: DaddyO

Hi, Lambchop—

Here we are in sunny L.A.—no thanks to our idiot pilot. The man had no idea what he was doing. I'm surprised we didn't wind up in Zanzibar! But once I voiced my concerns, I'm happy to say he shaped up and finally got us here.

Why didn't you tell us you were taking your cat with you on the cruise? Your mom had quite a scare when she thought she was missing. I, of course, knew all along there had to be some rational explanation for why we couldn't find her, but I phoned the police just to allay her fears.

Everything worked out fine in the end. Well, almost everything. One of the cops scuffed your wall with his nightstick on his way out. But fear not, lambchop. I'll clean it up.

By the way, we met your neighbor Lance. He and your mom really seemed to hit it off.

Well, it's been quite a day. Time to relax with my pipe. Did Mom tell you I started smoking one? It's a rare collector's item, the very same pipe Basil Rathbone smoked in the Sherlock Holmes movies! Lucky for me, I have a discerning eye and was able to snap it up for only a buck fifty.

Love & kisses,

Daddy

To: Jaineausten
From: Sir Lancelot
Subject: Such a Hoot!

I can't believe Prozac stowed away on board ship. Oh, well. At least now you'll have someone under eighty to hang out with.

I know I was supposed to tell your parents she was with you, but I met some friends for dinner after work, and by the time I got home, your dad had already called the police.

Your mom was so frazzled, I asked them over for cocoa and biscotti. Your parents are such a hoot. Do you know your father actually smokes a used pipe? What a contrast to my parents, who are about as much fun as dried oatmeal. In the meantime, your mom has invited me for dinner on Tuesday. What a sweetie!

Well, happy cruising! And if you meet any cute guys, give them my number. Haha.

XXX,

Lance

To: Jaineausten
From: Shoptillyoudrop
Subject: PS

Why didn't you tell me Lance was so attractive?
I wonder why a darling man like him isn't mar-
ried. Oh, dear. I've got to go open the window.
The smell of Daddy's pipe is driving me crazy.

Chapter 4

My neck was stiff as a board the next morning from sleeping without a pillow. Prozac, the spoiled brat, had hogged it all night and had only reluctantly abandoned it to perch on my chest and claw me awake for her breakfast.

I plucked her off and rolled over, only to see Samoa's manuscript looming on my night table, waiting to be edited. All nine hundred pages.

Oh, groan.

But I had to look on the bright side. Now that Samoa knew about Prozac, I'd be getting maid service. I could even ask him for another pillow.

See? There's always a silver lining.

Working on the Silver Lining principle, I got dressed and scooted over to the buffet, where I scored a divine breakfast of bacon, eggs, and cheese Danish for me and baked ham for Prozac. Countless calories later, I made my way up to the Sports Deck, where I ran a few brisk laps on the ship's jogging track. (Okay, so technically I didn't run any laps, but I did watch other people run laps. Does that count?)

Having burned off approximately three and a half calories, I headed over to the ship's computer room to check in with my parents and make sure they'd arrived safely. I'd recently bought a fancy new cell phone that did everything except brew coffee. One thing it did not do, however, was work on board ship. So I'd arranged with my parents to communicate with them via e-mail.

I found the computer room sandwiched between the ship's chapel and the Photo Studio. Several Webaholics were seated at a bank of computers getting their daily Internet fix.

One of them was Kyle Pritchard. Clad in a designer polo and Bermuda shorts, he was tapping away at his computer. At his feet was an attaché case, no doubt made of some endangered species. And spread out next to him were what looked like a bunch of financial statements.

"Hi, Kyle," I chirped.

"Hmmph," was his cheery reply.

Careful to put plenty of space between us, I settled down at a computer and tried to get an Internet connection. For some idiotic reason, I thought it would be free, as part of my "free, all-expenses-paid" cruise. But, alas, the helpful Holiday staffer on duty informed me that I wasn't about to be comped on e-mails.

"How much is it?" I asked.

"A buck fifty."

Gee, that wasn't so bad.

"A minute," he added.

Holy Moses. I made a mental note to keep my communications with my parents to a bare minimum. But after reading my e-mails I'm afraid I wasted valuable Internet minutes staring into space, agog at the thought of the cops charging into my apartment on a "catnapping" call.

It was so typical of Daddy, creating an uproar over nothing. I love him to pieces, but the man is a born crazymaker. I swear, he's caused more ulcers than pepperoni pizza and jalapeno chiles combined. How Mom has put up with him all these years, I'll never know.

Of course, Mom is not without a few quirks of her own. Not only is she constitutionally incapable of remembering my cat's name, she's probably the only person on the planet to move to Florida to be near the Home Shopping Channel, not for the weather or the oranges. Somehow she's convinced she gets her packages faster that way.

But I couldn't waste any more time dawdling over my e-mails. It was almost ten o'clock. Time for my first class of the cruise.

I have to confess I was a tad nervous.

When I'd first asked Paige how many people I could expect at my class, she'd replied:

"Oh, the big-name celebrities can attract hundreds. But someone of your caliber"—and there was no doubt she ranked me somewhere in the Three Stooges caliber of lecturer—"the most you can expect is fifty, maybe seventy-five."

Seventy-five people?? Gaack! To me that was a cast of thousands. The only other writing class I'd ever taught was at the Shalom Retirement Home, where I could count my students on the fingers of one and a half hands.

So it was with butterflies frolicking in my stomach that I raced back to my cabin to gather the seventy-five handouts I'd xeroxed for the class. Just my luck, the elevator took forever to show up, and when it finally did, it stopped at every floor.

Which meant that I was five minutes late when I finally came puffing up to the Galley Grill Restaurant, where the class was scheduled to take place. By now, those butterflies in my stomach were doing the conga.

My fear quickly turned to flop sweat when I walked into the restaurant.

There, seated at the tables that had been set up for the class, was a grand total of five students!

Five measly people? What happened to all the others?

I walked over to them, a sickly smile pasted on my face.

"Hello, there!" I said, my voice echoing in the cavernous restaurant. "Welcome to *Writing Your Life Story.*"

I prayed some latecomers would straggle in. Maybe some of them got held up in the elevator, like I did. Yes, I had to think positive thoughts. A whole bunch of them would probably come streaming in any minute now.

I introduced myself, and after explaining that I was no relation to the *Pride and Prejudice* Jane, I started passing out my handouts: a series of memory-stimulating questions about my students' childhoods, their jobs, their marriages, their children—in short, their lives.

If completed, I told them, the questionnaire would serve as a memoir to pass on to future generations. Or it could serve as a springboard to a longer, more ambitious project. All the while I chatted, I kept looking at the door hoping for somebody else to wander in. But alas, it looked like it was just me and my gang of five.

"So," I said, my smile now frozen in place, "why don't you all take turns and state your name and tell everybody why you decided to take this course.

"You, sir?" I asked a bushy-bearded guy with an opulent unibrow.

"I'm Max," he said. "Actually, I wanted to take Professor Heinmann's lecture series on his Arctic explorations, but, unfortunately, he had to cancel his cruise, so the class was called off."

So that's why Paige had offered me the job. I was a last-minute replacement.

"And Bingo was too crowded," he added, "so I wandered in here."

Great. Nothing like an enthusiastic student to get the ball rolling.

"I'm Rita," piped up the woman sitting next to him, a wiry-haired dame with small, squinchy eyes. "I'm president of the West Secaucus

Women's Reading Club, and I never miss an opportunity to hear an author speak."

Okay, at least this one had a vague interest in writing.

"On my last cruise," she announced proudly, "I saw Mary Higgins Clark."

"Really?" I said. "That must've been fun."

"Yes, she was fabulous. Just fabulous. Utterly spellbinding."

"Looks like I've got a tough act to follow. Haha."

"Humpph," she sniffed, clamping her arms over her chest, having clearly reached the conclusion that it would be a cold day in hell before I came close to filling Mary H. Clark's shoes.

"And what about you?" I asked a long-haired teenage boy, sitting at a table some distance away from the others. He couldn't hear my question, though, thanks to a pair of ear-buds stuffed in his ears. Totally oblivious, he nodded his head in time to music from his iPod.

"Young man!" I screeched.

"Who? Me?" he asked, popping out an earbud and peering at me through his fringe of bangs.

"Yes. What's your name?"

"Kenny."

I couldn't help wondering what a kid his age was doing in a class like this.

"Well, Kenny. Tell everybody why you're taking this class."

"My parents made me. They want you to help me with my book report on *The Scarlet Letter*."

Oh, for heaven's sake. First Samoa, and now this. It seemed like everyone on board had something for me to edit.

"I'm afraid I can't help you with that. This is a memoir-writing class. Feel free to drop out if you want."

I hated to lose him, but I was not about to play High School English Teacher.

"Nah," he said, "that's okay. There's nothing else to do on this dumb ship. Everybody here is like a hundred years old. Besides, my parents are paying me fifty bucks if I stay out of their hair for an hour."

I nodded wearily to my last two students, a sixtysomething couple, dressed in identical jogging suits—his blue, hers pink.

"We're David and Nancy Shaw from Seattle," the man said.

"And after forty years of marriage we're taking this cruise to renew our wedding vows," his wife chimed in.

Eyeing their matching jogging suits, wide, toothy grins, and Early Beatle bobs, I wondered if they'd always looked like each other, or if they were one of those couples who grew alike as the years went by.

"Anyhow," David said, "we thought it would be a wonderful idea to write down our memories to pass down to our children."

Alert the media! At last I had some people who actually wanted to write their memoirs.

"That's wonderful," I said, fighting the impulse to race over and kiss them.

I spent the next few minutes giving my students a mini-lecture on the principles of writing, trotting out the old "Show, Don't Tell" adage, urging them to go for specific memories rather than sweeping generalities.

"Just remember," I said, winding up my little chat, "what you write doesn't have to be perfect. Just keep writing. If you have difficulty, pretend you're writing a letter to a friend. Now let's get started. Everybody take out your pads."

"I don't have a pad," Kenny, my teen angel, sulked.

"I don't either," Max chimed in.

"I do," Rita said, with a virtuous sniff. "I always come prepared."

"You can write on the back of these," I said, tossing Max and Kenny some of my extra handouts.

Then, just as I was about to give them their first writing exercise, a tiny, white-haired woman drifted into the room. In her hands she carried a tote bag almost as big as she was.

"I'm so sorry I'm late," she said in a whispery voice.

"That's perfectly all right," I said, grateful for another mate on my motley crew. "What's your name?"

"I'm Amanda."

"Take a seat, Amanda. Here's a handout. We're just about to get started."

She sat down next to Max and smiled up at me. Thank heavens this one seemed pleasant.

"Now I want each of you to write about a first in your life. Your first date. Your first job. Your first day at school—"

"Can I write about my first colonoscopy?" Max asked. "It's where I met my second wife."

Talk about your love connections.

"That's fine," I said.

"Wait a minute," Rita piped up, poking a finger through her wiry curls to scratch her scalp. "Aren't you going to talk about your books?"

I refrained from telling her that, aside from *You and Your Garbage Disposal*, I had no books to talk about.

"No, Rita, I'm afraid not."

"But Mary Higgins Clark told us all about her books," she pouted.

"She sold her first book," she said, turning to the others to spread the news, "when she was widowed with five children!"

"How interesting." I forced myself to keep smiling. "But as I've already explained, this is a writing course."

"But I thought we'd be hearing stories," Rita whined.

"The only stories in this class will be yours," I said firmly. "Now, let's start writing, shall we?"

Rita's hand shot up.

"Are we going to be graded on penmanship?"

"There are no grades. Just write."

By now, I was *thisclose* to giving her a wedgie.

Nancy and David, the married couple, picked up their pens and started writing with gusto. The others were a tad less enthused. A lot of ceiling-staring and what I suspect was doodling ensued. But at last I saw pens crawling across paper. The writing process had begun.

The only one who wasn't writing was the old lady who'd come in after the class began. Instead, she'd taken a pair of knitting needles from her tote bag and was clacking away at what looked like an argyle sweater.

"Aren't you going to write anything, Amanda?" I asked. "It's fun once you get started. Just pretend you're writing a letter to a friend."

"Oh, no thank you, dear." Another sweet smile. "I've already written postcards to my friends back home."

"Don't you want to write about your life?"

"Oh, no, dear. Living it was enough for me."

Clearly the woman was not operating with a full deck, but I didn't care. I was just happy to see a smiling face.

For the next hour I continued to swim upstream with this bunch. Rita kept punctuating every assignment with tidbits from the Mary Higgins Clark files. In a stage whisper that could be heard all the way to Cabo San Lucas, she kept up a running commentary on how much more famous and entertaining Mary Higgins Clark was than yours truly.

At first I was gratified to see Kenny, the teenager, writing industriously, but when I peeked over his shoulder I realized he'd been busy perfecting his pornographic cartoon skills.

Max nodded off somewhere during the second writing assignment, his jackhammer snores echoing in the empty restaurant.

But on the plus side, you'll be happy to know that Amanda got a lot of work done on her argyle sweater.

My only shining lights were the married couple, who attacked their assignments with gusto.

At last, sixty painful minutes had come to an end. Not a nanosecond too soon.

"That's all the time we have for today," I said, hoping they couldn't hear the relief in my voice.

Kenny's hand shot up from the back.

"If there's homework, I'm not coming back tomorrow."

"There's no homework, Kenny. Just bring in what you wrote today, and we'll take turns reading aloud.

"See you all tomorrow!" I said, smiling my most appealing smile. As motley a crew as they were, I couldn't afford to lose a single one of them. "Any questions before we go?"

My sweet, white-haired lady raised her hand.

"Just one, Professor Heinmann," she said. "When are you going to tell us about your Arctic explorations?"

Chapter 5

Talk about your demoralizing experiences. I wanted nothing more than to trot over to the Tiki Lounge and bolster my sagging ego with a frosty margarita, but it was only 11 A.M. and I simply could not justify glugging down tequila at that hour of the morning.

Besides, I needed to keep my brain cells perky for their upcoming bout with Samoa's masterpiece.

So I trudged back to my cabin, where I found Prozac clawing on a cashmere sweater she'd dragged from my closet. Several pieces of my underwear were also scattered gaily on the cabin floor.

"I'm glad you've been having fun," I snapped, picking up the mess. "I've been through utter hell."

She scampered to my side and sniffed my ankles, then looked up at me with big green eyes that could mean only one thing:

So where are my snacks?

"Oh, for crying out loud, Pro, you ate enough ham this morning to feed an NFL quarterback. I'll bring you something later."

After scribbling a note to Samoa, asking him to pretty please bring me another pillow, I grabbed his manuscript and headed up to the pool deck. I found a spot in a secluded nook far from the frolicking crowds at the pool and settled down to do battle with *Do Not Distub*.

The less said about Samoa's opus the better. Let's just put it this way: I'd read better plots in my DVD manual. I spent the next few hours gritting my teeth in frustration, trying to decipher his miniscule scrawl.

All the while I could hear the happy shrieks of vacationers splashing in the pool.

For a mad instant, I considered tossing the whole ghastly mess overboard. But sanity prevailed and I slogged on, breaking only for a late lunch at the buffet (a heavenly roast beef panini, with just the weensiest chocolate chip cookie or three for dessert).

When at last my eyeballs were begging for mercy, I packed it in.

I was heading past the pool en route to my cabin when I heard someone call my name.

I turned and saw Emily Pritchard surrounded by her entourage: Kyle and his wife, Maggie; the formidable Ms. Nesbitt; and, of course, Adorable Robbie, who was looking particularly adorable in cutoffs and a sleeveless T-shirt.

With a jaunty wave, Emily beckoned me to join them.

As I made my way across the deck, I became aware of someone else in the Pritchard party. Cookie's boyfriend, Graham, dashing as ever in his nautical blazer, was standing at Emily's side. I hadn't seen him at first, so engrossed had I been in Robbie's cutoffs. But there he was, his hand resting most chummily on Emily's elbow.

How odd. I didn't think the hired dancers were allowed to fraternize with the passengers off the dance floor.

"Jaine, how lovely to see you." Emily beamed as I approached.

"Is that a manuscript you're carrying?" Nesbitt asked, catching sight of Samoa's masterwork in my arms.

I nodded wearily. I preferred to think of it as recyclable waste, but I suppose technically it was a manuscript.

"How marvelous!" Emily gushed. "We get to see your new book before anybody else."

Clearly she hadn't glommed on to the fact that I was not a famous author.

"Actually, this isn't my book. I'm editing it for a friend."

"How exciting! Isn't that exciting, everybody?"

"Oh, yes!" Maggie said, as Kyle stifled a yawn.

"*Do Not Distub*?" Nesbitt sniffed at the cover page as if it were a dead rat.

"And what have you guys been up to?" I asked, eager to change the subject.

"We've had such a fun day," Emily said. "We've been busy shopping."

Indeed, I looked down and saw they were all carrying shopping bags from the Holiday gift shop.

"I always like to treat everybody to little souvenirs of our cruises."

"Really, you shouldn't, Aunt Emily," Maggie said. "You're much too generous."

"I'll say," Kyle snapped, darting a none-too-subtle glance at the shopping bag dangling from Graham's wrist.

"Yes, my dear," Graham said in his velvety British accent. "It was much appreciated—but most unnecessary."

"It was my pleasure, Graham," Emily said, beaming up at him.

Up to this point, I'd been avoiding eye contact with Robbie. After the way he'd ditched me last night, I was determined to play it cool. But now I couldn't resist taking a peek at his face. And the minute I did, he hit me with his bad-boy grin.

Oh, rats. Why did he have to be so darn cute?

I stiffened my resolve to be cool and distant and unattainable.

But before I got a chance to give him the snub he so richly deserved, our peppy social director, Paige, got on the mike and announced that an exciting ice sculpture demonstration was about to begin.

Sure enough, I turned to see Anton seated at a table not far from us, with some ice picks and a big block of ice.

"Ooh, let's watch!" Emily said, with childlike enthusiasm.

"I'm afraid I can't, my dear," Graham said. "I've got some important business matters to attend to."

"What a pity." Emily's face fell.

"But I hope to see more of you later, sweet Emily."

Then he took her liver-spotted hand in his and kissed it. Wow, this guy was Cary Grant and Hugh Grant rolled into one.

Emily stared after him, dreamy-eyed, as he walked off.

Kyle was staring after him, too, with the wary, calculating look of a pit bull whose turf has just been threatened.

"C'mon," Ms. Nesbitt said, grabbing Emily's elbow. "Let's go see that ice sculpture."

"Yes, let's!" Maggie seconded, hustling us over to get a better view.

I tried to stay in the background, off Anton's radarscope, but unfortunately he saw me in the crowd and waved.

I smiled weakly and waved back.

I have to admit, Anton lived up to his own hype.

He wielded his ice picks with dramatic flair, picking and chipping away with the deftness of a neurosurgeon. Oohs and ahs erupted from the crowd as a bust of George Washington gradually emerged from the ice.

He finished with a flourish, and the crowd broke out in applause. He was so proud of himself, I was surprised he wasn't joining in.

It was then that I heard Robbie's voice in my ear.

"So how's it going?"

I turned to face him, and in spite of myself, I felt my heart do a two-step.

"You all set for Formal Night tonight?" he asked.

Oh, rats. I'd forgotten all about that. I still hadn't rented an outfit.

"Maybe afterward," he was saying, "we can go—"

I never did hear where Robbie wanted to go, because just then Anton, ignoring the people who'd gathered to chat with him, came barging between us.

Before I knew it, he had me cornered, his bright orange face just inches from mine. I watched help-lessly as Robbie shrugged in defeat and backed away.

"So, Jaine," Anton said, "when am I going to get to do *your* bust?"

Some other lifetime, mister.

"Seriously, doll, I'd love for us to get better acquainted." He smiled his version of a sexy smile, exposing a row of tobacco-stained teeth. "How about we rendezvous at my cabin tonight and I'll show you my instruments?"

Oh, wow. This guy was about as subtle as the bubonic plague.

"Sorry, Anton, I'm not interested."

"C'mon, baby. All the ship's employees fool around with each other. It's a nautical tradition."

"I'm afraid you'll have to carry on that proud tradition without me."

"Whattsa matter? You married? No problemo. I am too. What happens on board stays on board."

This said with a most nauseating leer.

"So how about it, sweetheart? You ready for a ride in my love machine?"

Oh, puh-leese. The only thing I was ready for was a barf bag.

"Sorry, Anton. Still not interested."

"That's okay, babe," he said, eyeing me like a sirloin in a butcher's case. "I like a challenge."

On that ominous note, he slithered away.

Alone at last, I looked around for Robbie, but once more, he was gone with the wind.

Chapter 6

"Omigod. I look just like my grandmother."
I was standing in the ship's Formal Wear rental shop, staring at my reflection in a three-way mirror. And I swear I was wearing the same outfit my grandmother wore to my cousin Joanie's wed-

ding: a long funereal black skirt, topped off with a matronly gold beaded twinset.

"Isn't this a little on the dowdy side?" I asked the saleslady helping me.

She was a tall, regal dame with her hair pulled back in a bun so tight I was surprised it wasn't coming out at the roots.

"You just need to accessorize it," she said with a brittle smile.

With what? A walker?

"Don't you have anything a little snazzier?"

"Not in your size, I'm afraid."

Well, excuuuse me for not being a size two.

"How about this one?" She held out a blob of dreary black lace.

"Wasn't Queen Victoria buried in something like this?"

"Very amusing." But like Queen Vicky herself, she did not look the least bit amused.

I stared at the gold-and-black number I was wearing and sighed. It was Dowdy Central, but at least it was better than Queen Victoria's shroud.

"So what's it going to be?" the saleslady asked, more than a hint of impatience in her voice. "You going to take it?"

I took it, all right. And paid a hundred and twenty bucks for the privilege.

I trudged back to the cabin with my granny outfit, stopping off at the buffet to pick up some poached salmon for Prozac. (Okay, and some peanut butter cookies for me. After an afternoon with *Do Not Distub*, I deserved them.)

When I opened my cabin door, I found Prozac pacing restlessly.

"Hi, sweetheart!" I crooned. "Mommy brought you dinner!"

She shot me a dirty look.

It's about time.

She practically knocked me over when I put her plate down, so eager was she to bury her pink nose in the stuff.

I was just about to hang my rented togs in my closet when I heard voices raised in Cookie's cabin next door.

Now I realize someone of your high moral caliber would never do something as tacky as eavesdrop, but I had no such compunctions. In no time flat, I had my ear glued to the wall.

"Are you nuts," I heard Cookie saying, "spending the day with the old lady like that? You know you're not supposed to socialize with passengers off the dance floor. You could get fired."

"Don't worry, darling." Graham's velvety British accent was unmistakable. "They'll never fire me. I'm very good at what I do."

"A little too good, if you ask me," Cookie huffed. "Why did you have to spend so much time with her, anyway?"

"Oh, sweetheart. She's a lonely old lady looking for a little companionship."

"Lonely? She's traveling with her own posse."

"Surely you're not jealous? Besides, I told her all about us."

"You did?" Cookie's voice began to soften.

"Absolutely. In fact, she gave me the name of a wonderful jeweler in Los Angeles who'll give us a good price on our wedding rings."

"Wedding rings?" she gasped.

"Of course, darling. That's what one usually buys when one gets married."

I have to admit, I was a tad surprised. After the way Emily had been mooning over Graham, it was hard to picture her playing matchmaker for another woman.

"Oh, Gray!" Cookie's voice was all melty now. "I wasn't sure. I mean, you always change the subject when I bring up marriage. I was beginning to think—well, no matter. I was wrong. I'm sorry I made such a fuss about the old lady. It's just that I hardly got to see you all day."

"That's why I'm here now, sweetheart," he purred. "To make up for lost time."

At which point, I heard the faint whine of bedsprings. Uh-oh. Looked like things were about to get X-rated. My cue to head off for the shower.

At home I like to soak away my cares in a strawberry-scented bathtub. No such luxury here on the Dungeon Deck. All I had was a shower the size of a phone booth. I spent the next ten minutes trying not to impale myself on the soap dish, all the while breathing in the heady aroma of Prozac's litter box.

I dried myself off with a threadbare towel not much larger than a dishcloth, then slipped into my robe and undies. I took my time moisturizing and perfume-spritzing and blow-drying my hair.

But then I could avoid it no longer. The moment of truth had arrived.

I took a deep breath and put on my rented togs.

"What do you think, Pro?"

She sniffed at the hem of my skirt much like she sniffs our garbage back home. Not a good sign.

I forced myself to look in the mirror, and once more I saw my grandmother looking back at me. Oh, crud. What would Robbie think when he saw me looking like a poster girl for PoliGrip?

I was standing there wondering what the penalty was for showing up on Formal Night in a pair of sweats when I heard a knock on the door.

"Who is it?" I called out cautiously.

"It's me. Cookie."

I opened the door and saw her leaning against my doorjamb in a short satin nightie.

"Oh, Jaine," she said, drifting into my cabin on a cloud of post-whoopie bliss. "I had to share the good news with you! Graham was just in my cabin."

So I'd heard.

"And he asked me to marry him!"

"That's wonderful! When's the happy day?"

"We didn't exactly set a date, but Graham said he knows a place were he can buy our wedding rings."

She plopped down on my bed and sighed.

"I can't tell you how happy I am. Before long, I'm going to be Mrs. Cookie Esposito Palmer III!"

I smiled weakly. Something told me Cookie might have been jumping the gun a wee bit. Just because Graham knew where to buy a wedding ring didn't mean he was actually prepared to slip it on her finger. And I wasn't sure I even bought that wedding ring story in the first place.

"Oh, dear." Cookie had come down off her cloud and was now eyeing my sorry outfit. "You've been to the rental shop, haven't you?"

I nodded miserably.

"I look awful."

"Well, you won't when I'm through with you. Wait here," she said, dashing out the door. "I'll be right back."

Minutes later she was back in my cabin with a professional make-up kit.

"I happen to be a whiz at this stuff," she said, dabbing foundation on my face.

She did not lie. The woman was a regular make-up Michelangelo. When she was through with me, my eyes were bigger, my lips were fuller, and for the first time in my life, I had cheekbones.

"Now, for your hair."

With what seemed like just a few spritzes of hairspray and some deftly placed hairpins, she wound my curls into a sexy Sarah Jessica Parkerish updo.

"Wow," I said, gazing at my reflection in the mirror. "This is such an improvement."

"Wait a minute. I'm not through."

With that she took a pair of dangly gold earrings from her pocket and put them in my ears.

The saleslady was right. Accessories did help. I didn't look half bad. I bet if I squinted my eyes and stood about three cabins away from the mirror, I'd even look skinny.

"Oh, Cookie. You really are my guardian angel."

"Don't be silly, hon," she said, wrapping me in a perfumed hug. "I'm sure you'd help me out if I was in a jam."

What neither of us knew at the time, of course, was that a jam of monumental proportions was right around the corner.

Chapter 7

I made my way across the dining room that night feeling pretty good about the new, improved me. My confidence was quickly shattered, however, by what I was about to see.

There, floating above the table next to mine, was a balloon reading, *Happy 100th Birthday, Ethel!* Sitting beneath the balloon was a frail old woman with pink cheeks and blue hair—Ethel, no doubt—wearing a button that said, *Kiss me. I'm 100!*

And that's not all she was wearing.

You guessed it. The exact same outfit as mine.

Yes, folks, I'd shown up dressed like a centenarian.

"Jaine, how lovely to see you," Emily said, catching sight of me.

Once more, the others had arrived before me and were seated with their cocktails. All dressed in non-rented togs far more fashionable than mine. Emily wore a spectacular lace gown, set off by a string of magnificent pearls I sure hope she was insured for. Maggie had on a champagne-colored halter dress that, although not particularly flattering to her generous upper arms, undoubtedly sported a designer label. Even Ms. Nesbitt had pulled out the stops and was wearing a tailored beige silk dupioni suit.

Kyle and Robbie both wore tuxes. And Robbie, I couldn't help but notice, was looking particularly spiffy, his green eyes startling against his tan, his sun-streaked hair still wet from a shower.

I smiled feebly and slipped into the vacant seat next to Emily, feeling about as stylish as the Volga boatman. I just prayed they hadn't noticed my centenarian fashion twin.

No such luck.

"Oh, Jaine," Ms. Nesbitt said, a wicked gleam in

her eyes. "You're wearing the same outfit as the hundred-year-old lady over there. Isn't that cute!"

I felt like shoving a dinner roll in her big fat mouth.

But I did not do any roll-shoving, because at that moment Graham Palmer III came gliding up to our table, once more channeling Cary Grant. I tell you, the man was born to wear a tuxedo.

"Good evening, everyone," he purred in a deep baritone.

"Guess what?" Emily's face glowed with pleasure. "I've invited Graham to join us for dinner."

Kyle looked up from his martini, not bothering to hide his irritation.

"But he's not assigned to our table."

"He is now, dear. That maitre d' said there'd be no problem if Graham sat with us for the rest of the cruise."

"The rest of the cruise?" Kyle washed down this news with a big gulp of his drink.

"I had him bring an extra chair to our table," Emily said.

Indeed, for the first time I noticed an empty chair at the table, two spaces down from Emily. I'd been so wrapped up in my fashion crisis, it hadn't registered before.

"Leona, dear," Emily said to Ms. Nesbitt, "why don't you take that chair, so Graham can sit next to me?"

Nesbitt blanched in disbelief, her face almost as white as her napkin.

"But I hate to trouble Ms. Nesbitt," Graham said smoothly. "I can sit over there."

"No!" Emily cried, like a child whose favorite toy has just been threatened. "I want you here next to me."

Jaw clenched tight in anger, Nesbitt grabbed her drink and changed seats, fuming as Graham slid into her vacated spot.

And Nesbitt wasn't the only one who was pissed. Kyle, clearly upset at having this interloper in our midst, polished off his martini and signaled the waiter for another.

Yes, indeedie, there was tension in the air.

And matters did not improve when the waiter returned to take our orders.

"Madame?" he asked, starting with Emily.

"The Steak Mexicana looks awfully good," she said.

It sure did. According to the menu, it was "broiled to perfection and smothered in onions and roasted red peppers."

"Good grief, Emily!" Ms. Nesbitt piped up, shaking her head. "You can't have the Steak Mexicana. Much too spicy."

"Oh, dear," Emily sighed. "I suppose I shouldn't."

And then Graham did the unthinkable. He contradicted Ms. Nesbitt.

"Oh, go ahead, Em," he said. "Get what you want."

"Do you really think so, Gray?"

"The steak's not that spicy, is it?" he asked the waiter.

"Not at all," the waiter replied.

"And besides," Graham said, with a wink, "you only live once."

"Yes," Emily said, clearly under his spell, "I think I'll have the steak."

Nesbitt seethed as Graham shot her a smug smile. Another victory for Graham in the Emily Wars.

The waiter proceeded to take the rest of our orders. Once again, due to my second-class citizenship, I was saddled with the chicken. But the others were under no such restraints, and I listened with envy as one after the other opted for red meat. Only Ms. Nesbitt held back, sticking with her ghastly vegetable plate.

Finally, the waiter trotted off, leaving our jolly party to converse with each other. Which was about as easy as that Sisyphus guy trying to roll a boulder up a hill.

What can I say? Conversation did not sparkle. Not with Nesbitt and Kyle in full-tilt snit mode.

Emily, however, seemed oblivious to the tension crackling in the air and chattered gaily about the day's activities.

"Graham and I won second prize in Scattergories! We had so much fun, didn't we, Gray?"

"So what exactly is it that you do for a living?" Kyle asked, clearly not interested in their Scattergories victory.

"Graham's a retired corporate executive!" Emily beamed.

"Fortunately," Graham said, "I was lucky with a few investments so I was able to retire young and pursue my love of cruising."

"Isn't it wonderful?" Emily beamed. "Gray loves cruising just as much as I do!"

"How nice," Maggie said, darting an anxious glance at her husband's rapidly draining martini glass.

"Where exactly did you work?" Kyle asked, not to be deterred from his cross-examination.

"The British Petroleum Corporation," Graham replied, with a cool smile. "For almost twenty years. I'll be happy to fax you my resume if you like."

"Touché, Graham," Robbie said, a twinkle in his eye.

To which Kyle muttered what I was certain was a hearty curse.

Thank heavens the waiter showed up just then with our appetizers. But alas, he eventually abandoned us to our own company, and the rest of the dinner slogged by under a thundercloud of tension, with Kyle and Ms. Nesbitt radiating hostility and poor Maggie watching helplessly as her husband downed one martini after another.

I, meanwhile, was trying desperately not to reach over and cut myself a hunk of Emily's Steak Mexicana. I was also busy trying to avoid eye contact with Robbie, who kept looking at me with that disconcerting grin of his.

But what bothered me the most, more than the tension, more than the lure of the forbidden Steak Mexicana and Robbie's lopsided grin, was the way Graham was cozying up to Emily, gazing deeply into her eyes and brushing her hand with the tips of his fingers.

He sure wasn't acting like a guy who had a fiancée waiting in the wings.

"Ready to take another spin on the dance floor?" Robbie whispered as we filed out of the dining room.

Just say no, I warned myself. *Do not get involved with a bad-boy heartbreaker. He walked out on you last night. He'll walk out on you again.*

"Please say yes," he said, sensing my hesitation. "If you don't, I'll have to dance with the battle-axe." He glanced over at Ms. Nesbitt, who was discreetly popping a Tums into her mouth.

I steeled myself against temptation, but all it took was one sniff of his baby powder, and the next thing I knew I was in his arms on the dance floor.

Obviously I missed class the day they passed out backbones.

Graham and Emily were dancing alongside us, Emily happily ensconced in Graham's arms. For a woman of her advanced years, she bore an uncanny resemblance to a high school teenager, batting her eyes and giggling at her date's bon mots.

Graham had his charm turned on full blast, earning every cent of what they paid him to keep the single ladies amused.

Cookie was up on the bandstand, still radiant from her earlier tryst, belting out old standards. Every once in a while Graham caught her eye and winked at her over Emily's shoulder.

What an operator.

Meanwhile, out in the audience, Kyle and Nesbitt were glaring at the happy couple, Kyle guzzling enough gin to open his own distillery.

"We're going to take a break now," the band-leader announced after Cookie wrapped up a lovely rendition of "Blue Moon." "But we'll be back in ten."

I started off the dance floor but Robbie pulled me back.

"Oh, let's not join the Gloomies," he said, eyeing Kyle and Nesbitt. "What do you say we take a walk out on deck?"

This time Sensible Me didn't even put up a fight.

"Sure," I managed to sigh.

It was a beautiful night, the kind you see in cruise-line commercials—mild and balmy with gazillions of stars in the skies. When you live with L.A.'s perpetual overhead gunk, you tend to forget how many of those twinkling babies actually exist.

We strolled along the deck, the moon glittering like diamonds on the water below. Talk about your Kodak moments.

What next, I wondered? Would Robbie turn to me and tell me how he'd always yearned to meet a freelance writer with generous thighs, and then take me in his arms and wrap me in a torrid embrace?

Apparently not.

"That was the dinner from hell," he said, not breaking stride.

Oh, well. It was all for the best he didn't make a pass at me. The last thing I wanted was to rush into things. (Who am I kidding? At that moment I wanted nothing more than to throw caution to the wind and plunge headlong into a frantic lip-lock.)

"I thought Nesbitt would have a cow when Aunt Em asked her to change seats."

"She was steamed, all right."

"Good for Aunt Em," he said. "I'm glad she's having fun. Poor thing's led a pretty sheltered life."

"She never married?"

"No. She had some big romance when she was very young, but it didn't pan out."

"I just hope she's not falling too hard for Graham. You know, he already has a girlfriend."

"I wouldn't worry about that. Underneath her ditsy ways, Aunt Em's pretty sensible. She's been on enough cruises to know that Graham is one of those men hired to dance with the single women. Surely she can't think anything serious is going to happen between them."

Obviously he hadn't Clue One about the self-deluding inner workings of a woman in love.

We stopped now and leaned against the rail, looking down at the moonlit waters below.

"Besides," Robbie said, "it's not Aunt Emily's love life I'm concerned about. It's yours."

"Mine?" I flushed.

"What's with you and that ice sculptor anyway?"

"Absolutely nothing," I assured him. "Nothing at all."

"I just thought from the way you two have been together . . ."

"No, Anton and I are definitely not an item."

"Any significant other back home?" he asked.

Play hard to get, I told myself. *Let him think he has some competition. Make up some guy you're seeing occasionally.*

"Aside from my cat, no."

Way to go, Jaine.

"Well, that's a relief." He inched just a tad closer. "So tell me about yourself. What do you do when you're not sailing the high seas?"

I told him about my career as a freelance writer, and my fondness for fine literature and crossword puzzles, carefully omitting my penchant for Chunky Monkey, *Cosmo* quizzes, and daytime TV.

"You go in for water sports?" he asked. "Sailing, scuba, that sort of stuff?"

And then the most outrageous lie popped out of my mouth.

"Oh, yes. I love it all."

Was I nuts? The only water sport I enjoyed on a regular basis was soaking in the tub.

"Really? Somehow I didn't think you were the type."

"Oh, but I am," I said, digging myself in even deeper. "I'm a real water nut."

Would somebody please shut me up?

And it looked like Robbie was about to do exactly that. Because just then he reached out and ran his finger along my cheek. I felt a jolt of excitement I hadn't felt in many a moon.

Much to my delight, he leaned in to kiss me. With any luck I would not be doing any talking for the next twenty minutes or so. Our lips were just about to meet when I heard:

"Hey, Jaine! I've been looking all over for you."

Phooey. It was Anton, hustling over to us.

"Look what I made you, babe!"

He held out a plate, and there in the center was a bright red jiggly blob.

"It's a rose carved out of Jello!"

"How nice," I managed to say.

"A precious flower for my precious flower."

Oh, puke.

"Hey, babe," he said, wedging his way between me and Robbie, "did I ever tell you about the time I carved the Eiffel Tower out of egg salad? Man, that was some tough job. I mean, you've got to get the egg salad really cold and not use too much mayo; otherwise it's too runny."

He proceeded to spend the next fifteen minutes giving a blow-by-blow description of the construction of his egg salad Eiffel Tower, his back to Robbie the entire time.

"What a fascinating story," Robbie said when he finally wound down.

"That's nothing. Wanna hear about the time I carved Moses out of chopped liver?"

"Some other time, Anton," I said. "I think I'll turn in now."

"Me too," Robbie chimed in.

With that, he grabbed my elbow and hustled me inside the ship, where we sprinted along the corridors, certain that Anton would soon be hot on our heels.

"In here," Robbie said, pulling me into the ship's game room, a wood-paneled enclave whose shelves were lined with board games and video rentals. Over at one of the tables, a bunch of kids were playing Uno.

We cowered in a corner, and seconds later we saw Anton rushing by.

"That guy is a human bloodhound," Robbie sighed.

So there we were in the game room, me holding a Jello rose, the kids at the table shrieking "Uno!" at the top of their lungs. No moonlight. No twinkling stars. No balmy breezes. The spell had definitely been broken.

"You know," Robbie said, "I think I really will turn in. I'm sort of tired."

"Me too," I lied.

What did I tell you? Dumped again.

I was dying to make a pit stop at the buffet, but I couldn't risk running into Anton. So I trudged back down to the Dungeon Deck with nothing more exciting to snack on than a Jello rose. Which I wasn't about to eat. Not after Anton had touched it.

Back in my cabin, Prozac sniffed at Anton's artwork disdainfully.

This is your idea of a midnight snack?

For once we were on the same wavelength.

With a weary sigh I got in my jammies and plopped into bed.

It was then that I noticed that Samoa had not brought me the pillow I'd requested. Most annoying. There were, after all, two beds in the cabin. There had to be another pillow for the second bed.

I made a mental note to have a stern talk with my steward-cum-novelist in the morning.

In the meanwhile, Prozac was perched on our one and only lumpy specimen. After copious pleading and belly rubbing I finally convinced her to relinquish her throne and lie on my tummy. Then I turned on the TV—believe it or not, my cabin actually had one—and zapped around until I found *Sleepless in Seattle* on the ship's movie channel.

Prozac and I spent the next hour and a half watching Meg Ryan and Tom Hanks fall in love. Rather, I watched. Prozac was snoring five minutes after the opening credits. I don't think she likes Meg Ryan. She doesn't like anybody as cute as she is.

Afterward I sat through a highly educational spiel on the many fun and exciting tourist attractions in Puerto Vallarta. None of which I could afford.

At about one-thirty, I turned off the light.

But sleep would not come. Visions of brownies danced in my head.

I could resist the lure of the buffet no longer. Surely Anton wasn't still roaming around looking for me. I threw on my raincoat, rolling up my pajama bottoms so they wouldn't show, and set out in search of empty calories.

The buffet was surprisingly busy. Apparently I wasn't the only late-night snacker on board. I scanned the room on Anton Alert, but much to my relief he wasn't there.

Five minutes later I was trotting back to my cabin with a brownie for me and roast turkey for Prozac. I'd just approached my cabin door when I caught a glimpse of Cookie slipping into Graham's cabin, a bright chartreuse sweater over her nightgown.

First Tom and Meg. Now Cookie and Graham. Love was all around me. I couldn't help but feel disappointed by the way Robbie had cut the evening short. True, the spell had been broken, but if he were really interested in me, would he have called it a night so quickly? I didn't think so.

Oh, well. I refused to let it get me down. We Austens are made of sterner stuff. Throughout the generations our motto has always been: *When the going gets tough, the tough get chocolate. With nuts, if possible.*

It worked for me.

YOU'VE GOT MAIL

To: Jaineausten
From: Shoptillyoudrop
Subject: Off to Universal Studios!

Good morning, honey! It's a beautiful day here in sunny Los Angeles, and Daddy and I are off to the Universal Studios tour. I hear they take you on the street from *Desperate Housewives*. I just love that show. All the housewives are so cute. Especially Felicity Parker Longoria!

Oops. Daddy's yelling for me to hurry. Must dash.

Lots of love from,

Mom

To: Jaineausten
From: Shoptillyoudrop
Subject: Desperate Housewife

We're back from Universal. What a fiasco! I never got to see any of the desperate house-wives. Or street they live on.

Would you believe Daddy tried to smoke his pipe on the tram?? The tour guide, a lovely young girl named Kimberly, told him as nice as you please that there was no smoking allowed. Which he should have realized since there was a big No Smoking sign at the front of the tram. But did Daddy cooperate? Of course not. He kept saying that the No Smoking sign didn't apply to pipes, especially one that was once owned by Basil Rathbone.

Kimberly tried to reason with him, but would he listen? Nooo! So before you could say, *Elementary, my dear Watson*, we were kicked off the tram! Right in front of the *Jaws* exhibit. Honestly, I felt like tossing your dad to the shark.

All the passengers sat there and gawked as two guards hauled us off in a security cart. Some Japanese people even took our picture! I think they thought we were part of the show. The guards dropped us off at the main entrance and warned us to never come back to Universal Studios or any of its affiliates for as long as we live.

I swear, I thought I'd die! If Daddy thinks I'm going sightseeing with him ever again, he's sadly mistaken.

Love from the original desperate housewife,

Mom

PS. One piece of good news. Before we got kicked off the tour, I got to talking with a darling young man visiting from Uzbekistan. I gave Vladimir your e-mail address. True, he's not exactly "geographically desirable," but who knows? He just might relocate to the United States one day.

To: Jaineausten
From: DaddyO
Subject: Such a Fuss!

I don't suppose you know any of the honchos at Universal, do you, sweetheart? I intend to write them a very stern letter of complaint.

Our prissy snip of a tour guide went crazy all because I happened to light my pipe on her stupid tram. Such a fuss. You'd think I'd taken out a loaded gun.

But you'll be proud to know your old daddy stood up for his rights and kept on smoking. I wasn't about to let some little girl barely out of diapers tell Hank Austen what to do. And besides, everyone knows "No Smoking" applies to cigarettes, not pipes.

Once she saw that I wasn't going to weaken under her tyranny, the little despot had the nerve to kick us off the tram—right in front of the shark from *Jaws*. Which I didn't mind a bit since I got to see the shark up close. Then two security guys showed up and gave us a ride back to the main entrance.

Your mother's making a big stink, but if you ask me, it all worked out for the best. Riding with the security guys, we got to see parts of Universal Studios that tourists never see! (How many people can say they rode past the *War of the Worlds* Porta Potties?)

Now I'm off to the hardware store to pick up paint for that scuff mark on your wall.

Love & kisses,

Daddy

To: Jaineausten
From: Shoptillyoudrop
Subject: Picasso's Eye

Dear Jaine—

Your father has gone to the hardware store to buy paint. He saw a tiny mark on your living room wall—so small you practically need a microscope to see it—and now he wants to paint over it. He insists one of the policemen did it with his nightstick, but if you ask me, Daddy probably did it himself bringing in the luggage.

I told him he'd never be able to match the color of your wall. But he insists he can. He says he has Picasso's eye for color. Ha! This from a man who can't tell his black socks from his blue.

Love from,

Mom

Chapter 8

I foolishly checked my e-mails the next morning on my way back from the breakfast buffet. And now my scrambled eggs were curdling in my tummy at the thought of Daddy running amok at Universal Studios. I'd be lucky if they ever let *me* in again.

Things didn't get much better when I ran into Samoa down in the Dungeon Deck.

"Hey, Samoa," I called out as he wheeled his supply cart along the corridor.

"Good morning, Ms. Austen. How are you today?"

"Fine. Great. Only I'd be a lot better if I had a pillow to sleep on. Didn't you get my note?"

"Yes, Samoa get note."

He smiled broadly, exposing several gold fillings.

"So?" I said. "There's a pillow missing from my cabin."

"Pillow not missing. Samoa has it."

"What are you doing with it?"

"Samoa likes sleeping with two pillows," he said, gracing me with another gold-laced grin. "Much more comfy."

Well, of all the colossal gall!

"I happen to like sleeping with *one* pillow," I pointed out, "and I don't have it."

95

"You have pillow in cabin. Old and lumpy. But you have one."

"Actually, my cat's using that one. So you need to bring me another," I said, shooting him the sternest look in my repertoire.

"Ah, yes. Your cat. We don't want anyone finding out about kitty in cabin and locking her in dark, cold cage, do we?"

Damn. He was playing the blackmail card again.

"No," I replied glumly.

"So Samoa keeps pillow," he grinned, "and everybody's happy!"

I knew where I wanted to shove that pillow right then.

"How you coming along with my book?"

"It's coming, Samoa. It's coming."

Grinding my teeth in frustration, I stomped back to my cabin, where I found Prozac snoring on the dratted pillow, having polished off a plate of baked ham I'd brought her earlier for breakfast.

I was so darn steamed with Samoa, I couldn't bring myself to work on his god-awful manuscript. Instead, I grabbed a tube of sun block and spent the next hour up on the pool deck doing crossword puzzles.

Heaven. Absolute heaven.

But like all good things it came to an end. At 9:45 I filled in a five-letter word for "devious devil" (no, it wasn't "Samoa") and put down my pencil.

It was time for my class.

• • •

When I showed up at my restaurant classroom, I was dismayed to see that my star pupils, Nancy and David, had gone AWOL. Drat. My anniversary couple were the only ones who'd expressed an actual interest in writing. How was I going to make it through the hour without them?

If only Rita, the irritating Mary Higgins Clark fanatic, had been the one to take a powder. But, no. There she was at the front table, scowling at me. Max the snorer was there too, as was Kenny, the teen slacker, his iPod still glued to his ear.

Even Amanda the knitter had returned. I must admit I was surprised to see her.

I thought I'd made it clear to her that I wasn't Professor Heinmann.

"You realize I won't be talking about the North Pole?" I asked her.

"That's all right, dear," she said, needles clacking.

"And you still want to take the class?"

"You have so few students," she tsked, her eyes round with pity. "I thought I'd stay and keep you company."

"Mary Higgins Clark had three hundred people show up at her lecture," Rita happily informed us.

"So," I said, putting a firm stop to the Mary Higgins Clark chatter, "who wants to read their essay?"

Rita's hand shot up.

I nodded at her grudgingly.

"Okay, Rita. Let's hear it."

But she did not begin reading. Instead she clamped her arms across her chest and said, with no small degree of belligerence, "I looked you up on Google."

"Oh?"

"And you had only one entry. About the Golden Plunger Award you won from the Los Angeles Plumbers Association."

"Your point being?"

"I don't see how the cruise line can hire a lecturer who shows up only once on Google. Mary Higgins Clark has seventeen pages on Google. That's more than Albert Einstein," she confided to the others.

"So, Rita, do you have anything to read?" I asked, barely resisting the impulse to strangle her.

"Nope." She shrugged. "I never got around to writing anything."

"Well, who *does* have something to read?"

I scanned the room and saw that Kenny, my teen slacker, was clutching a piece of paper. I blinked back my surprise. Had he actually put pen to paper?

"Kenny, how about you?"

"Okay, sure."

He brushed back a hunk of hair from his eyes and began reading.

"*The Scarlet Letter* is this really stupid story

about a lady who has to wear the letter *A* on her chest—I don't get it. All she did was sleep with a married man. I mean, half the kids in my class have moms who've done that—"

"Um, Kenny, you were supposed to write about a first in your life. Not a book report."

"Yeah, well. This is a first. First time I ever wrote a book report."

Hating to squash what little initiative this kid seemed to possess, I let him read the whole thing. Which turned out to be little more than a paragraph, lamenting the shortcomings of both Nathaniel Hawthorne and Ms. Tippit, his English teacher.

"Very interesting perspective," I commented lamely when he was through.

Now that the ice had been broken, Max's hand shot up.

"I'll read mine."

After a phlegm-filled clearing of his throat, he proceeded to read us a rather graphic account of his first colonoscopy, wherein he met his second wife. You may or may not be interested to learn that while the colonoscopy worked out just fine, the marriage did not.

"Very colorful," I said when he was finished. "Lots of vivid descriptions—maybe a little too vivid of your bowel movements—and watch out for redundant expressions like 'fatso porker' when describing your ex-wife.

"Anyone else have anything to say about Max's story?"

I looked around, hoping that a lively discussion would ensue, but was met with a wall of silence.

Oh, dear. There were no more stories to read. No more comments to make. The class was over ten minutes after it had begun. What the heck was I supposed to do for the next fifty minutes?

And then a miracle happened. Just as I was ready to start lecturing on *The Scarlet Letter*, David and Nancy came rushing into the room in matching mauve jogging suits. Never in my life was I so happy to see two people. (Aside from Ben & Jerry, of course.)

"Sorry we're late," David said. "We were busy checking the decorations for the chapel."

"Tonight's the night we're renewing our wedding vows," Nancy chimed in, flushed with pleasure.

"That's wonderful!" I said. "And don't worry about being late. You're just in time to read us your essays."

"I hope they're okay," Nancy said.

"I'm sure they'll be fine." I smiled confidently. Whatever they wrote would seem like gold compared to Max's colonoscopy saga.

"I'll go first," David said, "if that's okay with you, honey."

"Of course, dear," Nancy replied.

He took out some papers from his jacket pocket,

shook them out with a flourish, and began reading.

" 'Our First Date.' By David Shaw. I'll never forget my first date with my wife. It was a warm summer night, and I borrowed my dad's Impala to take Nancy to a drive-in movie. We saw the eight o'clock show of *Rebel Without a Cause*—"

Nancy, who'd been smiling up at him lovingly, held up her hand.

"Wait a minute, honey. It wasn't *Rebel Without a Cause*. It was *East of Eden*."

"It was? That's funny. I could've sworn it was *Rebel Without a Cause*. My mistake, sweetie."

He smiled at her and started reading again.

"After the movie, we went to Mel's Malt Shop, where we had burgers and fries."

"No, honey," Nancy interrupted. "We had cherry pie à la mode."

A twinge of irritation began to show on David's face.

"Burgers, pie à la mode. What's the difference? It was a snack, right?"

He picked up his paper and began reading again.

"Afterward, we drove out to—"

But we weren't about to learn where they went afterward.

"How could you forget we had cherry pie à la mode?" Nancy pouted. "Why else do you think I order it every year on our anniversary?"

"I don't know. I thought you just liked it. Honey,

let's not nitpick. All I know is that I fell head over heels in love with you the minute I rang your doorbell and saw you standing there in your pink angora sweater and matching poodle skirt."

He turned to the class and beamed.

"She was the prettiest girl in Fairfield High."

"Wait a minute!" Nancy said, eyes narrowed. "I wasn't wearing a pink angora sweater and poodle skirt. I didn't even own a poodle skirt. The only one in school who had a pink poodle skirt was Peggy Ann Martin. You fell head over heels in love with Peggy Ann!"

David scratched his head, puzzled. "I could've sworn it was you."

Uh-oh. I didn't like where this train was heading.

"You see, class," I butted in, "that's why details are so very important in your writing. In fact, maybe this would be a good time to go over those writing tips I gave you last session."

But my star pupils were not about to be distracted.

"I can't believe I broke up with Jeffrey Muntner to go out with you," Nancy snapped.

"You were dating Jeffrey Muntner?" David's eyes grew wide with disbelief. "You never told me that."

"Of course I did."

"No wonder you were so chummy with him at the reunion! I suppose you regret not sticking with him now that he's a big time used car dealer."

"Well, if I'd known you were head over heels in love with Peggy Ann Martin, maybe I would have."

"Maybe you should have. Maybe you should call him right now."

"Maybe I will!"

At this juncture, Amanda, who'd put down her knitting to watch the drama, commented to Max, "Such an interesting play! And such talented actors!"

"Maybe we should just call off renewing our vows." By now David was shouting. "I always thought it was a pretty silly idea anyway. Once was enough."

"Now you're telling me you didn't even like our wedding."

"Not with your Uncle Ed getting drunk and falling face-first into the punch bowl, no, I didn't!"

"How about we go over those writing tips?" I said, trying desperately to stop the train wreck.

But, alas, it could not be stopped.

"And for your information," David shouted, his face as mauve as his jogging suit, "I hate cherry pie à la mode!"

"I want a divorce!" Nancy wailed.

"Fine by me!"

Omigod, their forty-year marriage was falling apart right before my eyes. All because of a writing assignment I'd given them. The next thing I knew they were storming out of the class.

What the hell was I supposed to do now?

"So, Rita," I said, "why don't you tell us some more about Mary Higgins Clark?"

Somehow the class limped to a close.

You'll be pleased to know that I did not race over to the Tiki Lounge to calm my shattered nerves with a frosty margarita. No, I did the sensible thing and ordered a Bloody Mary out on the pool deck. So much healthier—the tomato juice, you know.

I sipped it while stretched out on a deck chair, waiting for my nerve endings to stop doing the cha-cha.

The warm sun felt good on my body, and after a while the rhythmic lap of the waves lulled me to a near naplike state. Yes, I was definitely mellowing out.

That is, until I looked up and saw Anton striding toward me in a T-shirt and cutoffs, his nose stud glinting in the sun.

Good lord. The man was wearing black socks with sandals. If Lance could see him, he'd go into cardiac arrest.

Thanks to the vodka sloshing around in my veins, I didn't have the energy to run for cover. Instead, I took a healthy slug of my Bloody Mary, hoping it would numb me to the slimy passes to come.

But much to my relief, Anton did not come on to me.

"You won't believe what happened!" he huffed, plopping down onto the deck chair next to mine. "Somebody stole my ice picks."

"Omigosh. How? Did they break into your cabin?"

I certainly hoped there wasn't a burglar running loose. The last thing I needed was someone barging into my cabin and discovering Prozac.

"Nobody broke into my cabin," Anton assured me. "Or my supply case, either. The lock hadn't been broken. My guess is that someone stole them yesterday after the demonstration when I was talking to you."

I remembered how he'd left his table unattended to ply me with his dubious charms.

"I put my tools away in a hurry and didn't bother to count them, but this morning I discovered two of them were missing."

He looked around, scowling.

"Damn passengers. They steal everything that isn't bolted down. Towels. Salt shakers. And now my ice picks. What a bunch of lowlifes."

This from a guy whose T-shirt said, *Love Instructor. First Lesson Free.*

"Mind if I have a sip?" he asked, eyeing my Bloody Mary.

Without waiting for a reply, he whipped it from my hand and polished it off in three gulps.

"Thanks," he said, wiping his mouth with the back of his hand. "I needed that."

So did I, buster. Now how about buying me another?

"So, Jaine, what did you think of my Jello rose?"

That lecherous look was creeping back in his eyes.

"Very nice, Anton. But you really shouldn't have done it."

"Just trying to win you over, babe," he winked.

"I already told you, Anton. I'm not interested."

"And I already told you, doll. I like a challenge."

Okay, time to skedaddle.

"Gotta go," I said, hauling myself up from my chair.

"Aw, c'mon, Jaine. What's it going to take to get you in the sack?"

"General anesthesia."

And with that, I scooted off to freedom.

Anton's repulsive offer was almost enough to make me lose my appetite. Almost, but not quite. Somehow my taste buds managed to rally and were now begging to be fed. So I headed off to the buffet for a much-needed bite to eat.

I was navigating one of the ship's many serpentine corridors when I saw Paige approaching from the opposite direction. The normally perky, peppy social director was looking neither perky nor peppy at the moment. *Au contraire.* Her mouth was set in a grim line as she marched along, making notes on her clipboard.

She couldn't possibly have heard about what happened with David and Nancy so soon, could she?

Nevertheless, perhaps it was best I stay off her radarscope.

I decided to duck into a nearby jewelry shop and pretend I was interested in one of their overpriced baubles, but it was too late. Paige had already spotted me.

"Jaine!" she called out. "We need to talk."

I mustn't panic. Just because she looked like she wanted to throttle someone didn't necessarily mean that someone was me. There were all sorts of things she could be steamed about. Maybe she ran out of Bingo cards. Or Ping-Pong balls. Or perky pills. Think positive, I told myself, as she tapped her pencil in an angry staccato on her clipboard. She probably had no idea of the marital disaster that had erupted in my classroom.

"I heard all about what happened in your class today," she snapped.

So much for positive thinking.

"That little tiff between Mr. and Mrs. Shaw?" I said, putting on my most innocent face. "Really, Paige, it sounds a lot worse than it was. Why, I bet by now they've already kissed and made up."

"Mr. Shaw has just moved into a separate cabin."

By now, icicles were forming in the atmosphere above us.

"Oh, dear. Is there anything I can do?"

"Short of finding them a divorce attorney, I don't think so. The Shaws, along with fifteen family members, are disembarking the ship tomorrow in Puerto Vallarta."

Oh, crud.

"You realize of course, that's seventeen passengers we'll never see again."

"I bet for a company as big as Holiday Cruise Lines, seventeen people is just a drop in the bucket."

"Here at Holiday," she said, trotting out a gag from the employees' handbook, "every passenger is our Number One concern.

"Needless to say," she added, "the wedding renewal ceremony has been canceled. And since we were comping the Shaws on their wedding cake, we think it's only fair that you pay for half. Don't you agree?"

Of course not! I wanted to shriek. Holiday Cruise Lines was a multi-million-dollar operation; I was a struggling freelance writer with enough unpaid bills to start a bonfire.

But wimp that I am, I said yes of course, it was only fair.

Besides, how much could half a cake cost, anyway?

(Two hundred bucks, as I was to learn, to my horror, when I got my bill at the end of the cruise.)

"Before I let you go, Jaine, I just want to say that never in all my years as a cruise director has something like this happened."

And with that she let out a series of indignant sneezes.

"Gosh, I hope you're not catching a cold," I said, eager to change the subject.

"Of course not. I never catch colds. It feels like my allergies are acting up."

She sneezed again. "If I didn't know better, I'd swear there was a cat on board ship."

"Ha ha!" I said, feigning hilarity. "What a crazy idea. Well, must run and do some prep work for my next class. Ciao for now!"

With a jaunty wave, I dashed off, praying she hadn't noticed the generous coating of cat hairs clinging to my slacks.

Down in the Dungeon Deck, I flung myself on my pillowless cot, wishing I could ditch this cruise from hell and disembark with the Shaws in Puerto Vallarta.

But as you know, we Austens are made of sterner stuff. No way would I walk out on my contract. That's because I had integrity, because I had principles, and most important, because I couldn't afford the airfare back home.

Lying there in a miserable lump, I leafed through the ship's notices that had accumulated in the little plastic docket outside my door.

There among the flyers from the ship's boutiques was a handwritten note from Emily, asking me to please join her and her "little family" in her suite at 6 P.M. for cocktails and hors d'oeuvres.

At least I was still in Emily's good graces.

I checked my watch. Five more hours until the hors d'oeuvres kicked in.

In the meanwhile, it was time to make that proverbial leap from the frying pan into the fire. Yep, ever the glutton for punishment, I picked up a pencil and returned to my chores in the literary gulag known as *Do Not Distub*.

Chapter 9

Emily's cocktail party was in full swing—and, much to my delight, Robbie had whisked me aside the minute I came in the door, leading me out onto the balcony.

It was raw and damp in the dusky night air. Gulls were circling above and storm clouds were gathering. But I didn't care. I was alone with Robbie and that's all that mattered.

"Let me give you my jacket," he said, putting his blazer over my shoulder.

I reveled in the warmth from his body.

"I wanted to get you alone, Jaine, because I have something to tell you."

He looked at me with what I could swear was a reasonable facsimile of love in his eyes.

"Ever since I first saw you, I've really been attracted to you."

"Oh, me too!" I blurted out before I could stop myself.

And then he took me in his arms. This was it. The big kahuna. The moment I'd been fantasizing about when I should have been editing Samoa's manuscript.

But just as he was about to kiss me, a bird came swooping down between us. A strange, ugly black bird with long furry feathers.

I cried out in horror as it spread its enormous wings. I tried to back away, but its feathers were in my nose smothering me.

"Help!" I screamed. "Somebody help me!"

Where the heck was Robbie? And why wasn't he helping me?

The bird glared at me through bulging eyes and then opened its enormous beak. Omigod. It was going to peck me to death. I was going to be human birdkill!

But then the bird did the strangest thing: it meowed.

It was then that I woke up and realized I wasn't at Emily's cocktail party but back in my own cabin, Prozac's tail draped over my nose.

I'd fallen asleep, Samoa's manuscript pages scattered around me on the bed. It may have stunk as a novel, but it was one heckuva sedative.

I checked my watch. Six o'clock! I was late for the cocktail party.

With no time to shower, I threw on some slacks and a silk blouse and tore over to Emily's suite.

Batting down a cowlick that had cropped up during my nap, I knocked at her door. Nesbitt answered it, all dolled up in an Aunt Bea floral dress and prison-warden support hose.

"You're late," she muttered, peering at me through her horn-rimmed glasses.

So nice to see you, too.

She led me inside and I gazed in awe at the plush surroundings. Cushy carpeting, thick damask drapes, plasma TV, and not one but two sofas flanking a coffee table as big as my bed. What a palace compared to my jail cell.

Emily was seated on one of the sofas next to Graham, still Mr. Debonair in his nautical blazer and snow-white shirt. By now I was not surprised to see the suave Brit as part of Emily's "little family."

Seated across from them on the opposite sofa were Kyle and Maggie—Kyle glaring daggers at the happy couple, while Maggie scarfed down hors d'oeuvres, eyes darting nervously to Kyle's ever-present martini glass.

Ms. Nesbitt plopped down next to them and joined Kyle in his glare-a-thon.

"Jaine!" Emily beamed. "So happy you could make it."

The normally makeup-free Emily was wearing lipstick. And mascara, too. And it looked like she'd been to the ship's beauty salon; her gray curls had been sprayed to concrete perfection.

"Sit here," she said, patting an armchair next to her.

"What can I get you to drink, Jaine?" Robbie asked.

I turned and noticed him for the first time, looking quite yummy in a blazer and chinos. He was standing in front of a black onyx bar, complete with silver ice bucket and martini shaker. Good heavens. I'd died and gone to Art Deco heaven.

"A white wine, please."

"Coming right up."

"Care for an hors d'oeuvre?" Maggie held out a plate of dainty toast rounds topped with what I was certain was caviar.

"It's beluga," she added.

Kyle rolled his eyes.

"As if she'd know the difference."

Okay, so he didn't really say that. But I could tell that's what he was thinking.

"And these are gravlax," Maggie said, pointing to some pink fishy stuff.

Let's see. I had a choice between black fishy stuff and pink fishy stuff. Hadn't these people ever heard of Velveeta on a Ritz? Stifling a sigh, I went for the black stuff.

Yuck. It was every bit as fishy and slimy as I'd imagined. At last I'd discovered something worse than tofu.

"Delicious," I said, faking a smile.

I scanned the room for something vaguely edible and spotted a bowl of fruit next to me on an end table. My eyes lit on a shiny red apple. Normally, fruit is not my go-to snack, but it quickly zooms to the top of my list when my other choices are of the slimy fish variety. That apple looked darn good. So as Emily started chattering about an action-packed shuffle-board game she and Graham had played that afternoon, I reached over and grabbed the apple.

Just as I was about to bite down on it, Nesbitt shrieked, "What do you think you're doing?"

All eyes swiveled to me and the apple in my mouth.

"You mustn't eat that, dear!" Emily cried.

"The fruit's fake," Nesbitt said.

I quickly tossed it back in the bowl.

"I bought it two years ago on a cruise down the Mediterranean." Emily smiled at the memory. "Such a wonderful cruise, wasn't it, Leona?"

"Yes," Nesbitt said. "*That* cruise was nice. It was just the two of us, if I recall," she added, shooting Graham a particularly filthy look.

Oh, Lord. I'd almost chomped down on a precious memento! How mortifying. Hadn't Lucy done something just like this at Ricky's boss's house? The next thing I knew I'd be blacking out my teeth and stomping grapes with my bare feet.

"I'm so sorry," I said.

"Don't feel bad," Robbie said, handing me my wine. "I once spent twenty minutes trying to peel the banana."

How sweet that he was trying to make me feel better. Not so with the charming Ms. Nesbitt.

"I hope you didn't leave any bite marks," she said, examining the apple.

I cringed in shame, wishing I were back down with the peasants in the Dungeon Deck.

But my humiliation was quickly overshadowed by the bombshell that was about to explode.

"Attention, everybody," Emily said, tapping a knife against her wineglass. "Graham and I have an announcement to make."

Kyle took a deep gulp of his martini, and Ms. Nesbitt blinked behind her horn-rimmed glasses.

"Why don't you tell them, Gray?" Emily smiled coquettishly at Graham.

"I'd be delighted to, darling," he said, flashing her a smile almost as white as his shirt.

"My beloved Emily and I," he announced, "are going be married."

Apart from a strangled gasp from Ms. Nesbitt and the glug-glug of gin sluicing down Kyle's throat, the silence was deafening.

"Isn't anyone going to say anything?" Emily looked around at her family.

Maggie, who had been sitting with an hors d'oeuvre frozen in her hand, came to life first.

"Congratulations!" she managed to say, with a stunned smile.

"Yes, congratulations," Robbie echoed. He, too, looked like he'd just been bopped with a baseball bat.

Kyle and Nesbitt, unable or unwilling to comment, remained etched in granite.

"Show them your cuff links, Gray."

Graham shot the French cuffs on his shirt, displaying a set of dazzling diamond-studded cuff links.

"An engagement present from your aunt," he said, with a smug smile.

"They were so lovely," Emily said, "I couldn't resist.

"Look at the time!" she said, jumping up. "If you'll all excuse me, I'll just go to the powder room, and then we'll head off to dinner!"

She trotted off to her bathroom, blissfully unaware of the hostility crackling around her.

The minute she was gone, Kyle slammed down his martini glass and hissed at Graham, "I knew you were trouble from the get-go, mister. But you won't get away with it. You hear me? You won't get away with it."

I, for one, would not want to be staring into his face, now purple with rage. But Graham did not seem the least bit perturbed.

"Try and stop me," he said airily.

"Believe me, I will. No matter what it takes."

"Lots of luck. But I doubt anything will stop Emily from marrying me," Graham said, buffing his new cuff links on the arm of his blazer. "She's in love, don't you know? Oh, and by the way, once we tie the knot, Kyle, you won't ever get your hands on her money again. So you'd better kiss your Town & Country lifestyle good-bye.

"And you, Ms. Frostbite," he said, nodding to Ms. Nesbitt, "you'd better start checking the want ads. I have a feeling Emily won't be needing your services anymore."

"That's what you think, you gold-digging bastard," Nesbitt hissed. The woman was *thisclose* to garroting him with her support hose.

But all further threats and counterthreats were stifled as Emily came out of the bathroom.

"Is everybody ready?" she asked.

For dinner? Not so much.

For thermonuclear war? You betcha.

How awkward was dinner? Let's just say it made *Who's Afraid of Virginia Woolf* look like an episode of *The Waltons*. The tension was so thick you could cut it with a steak knife, an implement I was once again denied due to my second-class citizenship.

But for a change I wasn't thinking about food. (Not much, anyway. My scalloped potatoes were to die for.)

I had to tell Emily the truth about Graham and Cookie. But how? I couldn't very well say, *Please pass the salt, and by the way, your cheating bum of a fiancé already has another tootsie waiting in the wings.* Somehow I'd have to think of a way to get her alone.

When dinner finally staggered to a close, Emily insisted we see the headlining act in the ship's Grand Showroom, a magician called The Great Branzini.

"I just love magicians," she exclaimed. "And this Branzini fellow is supposed to be the toast of Las Vegas."

As much as I wanted to take a break from my dysfunctional dinner companions, I agreed to go, hoping I'd be able to wrench Emily away from Graham and tell her the truth about her intended. Who, incidentally, looked none too happy at the prospect of my company. The last thing Graham wanted was me hanging around. I knew too much. Way too much. And thanks to my eavesdropping, I was an earwitness to what some folks might consider a proposal of marriage.

Minutes later we were all trooping over to our seats in the Grand Showroom.

Kyle sat at the far end of our group, as far as possible from Graham; Maggie sat next to him, followed by Nesbitt, and then the lovebirds.

"You go first," Robbie said, waving me ahead when the two of us were left standing in the aisle.

Either he was being gallant or he, too, was unwilling to sit next to his aunt's betrothed.

I plopped down in the hot seat next to Graham, Robbie on my other side. Graham barely acknowledged my existence, too busy whispering sweet nothings to Emily. The rest of us sat in stony silence as we waited for the curtain to go up.

I tried making conversation with Robbie, but he answered in monosyllabic grunts. Throughout dinner, he'd been distracted, looking at his aunt with worry in his eyes. And frankly, I couldn't blame him. There was trouble in Pritchard City, no doubt about it.

Having given up on Robbie, my mind wandered to my nightly pit stop at the buffet. I was debating between chocolate chip cookies and brownies— brownies had a slight edge—when suddenly I heard a woman shrieking:

"You miserable sonofabitch!"

I turned to see Cookie storming down the aisle in one of her spangly show gowns.

She screeched to a halt at our row.

"I just heard the news," she spat at Graham. "You're marrying *her?*"

She eyed Emily in disbelief.

"Yes, Cookie," Graham replied, cool as a cucumber. If the opposite of nonplussed was plussed, he was plussed to the max. "Emily and I have decided to tie the knot."

"But you can't marry her!" Cookie wailed. "You're engaged to me!"

"He's engaged to me!" she repeated to Emily. "I swear. He gave me half a heart." She lifted her pendant and showed it to Emily and everybody else in the Grand Showroom. "He promised he'd marry me!"

By now, two security guards had descended on her.

"Leave me alone," she said, swatting at them. But these guys were as big as refrigerators. They hoisted her by the elbows and began hauling her back up the aisle.

"You miserable sonofabitch!" she screamed at Graham as they carted her away. "You don't deserve to live!"

A buzz of excited chatter filled the air in the wake of her exit, everyone yapping about the dramatic scene they'd just witnessed.

The Great Branzini sure had a tough act to follow.

"I knew all along your precious Graham was no good!" Kyle crowed. "The man is a con artist, Aunt Emily!"

"He's just out for your money!" Nesbitt chimed in.

Emily turned to Graham and looked at him questioningly, her face pale.

But he didn't miss a beat.

"You mustn't believe Cookie," he said, smooth

as silk. "She's mentally unbalanced; anyone can see that. We're not engaged. Never were. We're just good friends, that's all. Everything else is all in her imagination."

Okay, I could sit through this claptrap no longer. Time to speak up.

"That's not true, Emily," I protested. "Graham *is* engaged to Cookie. I heard him tell her he'd buy her a wedding ring."

Graham whirled on me, his gray eyes cold as steel.

"I don't know what you think you heard, Jaine, but I never proposed to Cookie. She and I are just good friends."

"Emily," I said, "I swear I heard—"

Emily held up her hand to stop me.

"No more, Jaine. I'm sure you must be mistaken. If Graham says he didn't ask Cookie to marry him, I believe him."

She gazed up at him and smiled serenely.

And at that moment, I realized Emily knew exactly what she was getting into. She knew Graham was a gold digger, and she didn't care. She'd tossed her good sense out the window and put her heart and money on the line.

Just another hapless victim in the game of love.

YOU'VE GOT MAIL

To: Jaineausten
From: DaddyO
Subject: A Perfect Match!

Well, lambchop, your old Daddy did it again!

I just finished painting over that spot on your wall, and if I do say so myself, I did a terrific job. It was a perfect match. You'd never know there was ever a scuff mark!

Love and hugs,

Daddy

To: Jaineausten
From: Shoptillyoudrop
Subject: What a Klutz!

Oh, Lord. Your father has gone and done it again!

I knew I should've never let him paint that scuff mark. Not only does the paint clash with the color on your wall, but now he's gone and spattered some of it on your beautiful hardwood floor! What a klutz!

Sorry I can't write more now. Lance is coming for dinner and I've got to check my pot roast.

Love from,

Your frazzled Mom

To: Jaineausten
From: DaddyO
Subject: One Tiny Problem

Hi, Lambchop—

I forgot to mention a tiny problem that cropped up when I painted that spot on your wall. A bit of the paint spattered onto your hardwood floor. But I'll just get it off with some paint remover, easy-sneezy, no problemo.

By the way, did your mom tell you she invited Lance over for dinner tonight? Such a production! You'd think the Pope was coming. All I can say is it's a good thing I've got my trusty pipe to relax with.

XOXO,

Daddy

To: Jaineausten
From: Shoptillyoudrop
Subject: PS from Mom

PS. When was the last time you cooked a meal in your oven, sweetheart? When I opened it to put in the roast, I found an umbrella.

Chapter 10

I was jarred awake the next morning by a commotion next door in Cookie's cabin. I did not need to put my ear to the wall to hear footsteps stomping, drawers slamming, and Cookie shouting, "I swear I don't have them!"

Then the cabin door banged shut and all was quiet. Except for the faint sounds of Cookie sobbing. Oh, dear. Something was obviously very wrong.

I needed to find out what I could do to help. But first I had to tend to Prozac, who had assumed her morning position on my chest, clawing me for her breakfast.

I staggered out of bed to get her some roast beef I'd had the foresight to pick up last night at the buffet bar. I'd stored it in the cabin's minifridge, along with the $6 Cokes and $20 half bottles of wine. (Apparently beverages were not included in my free cruise, a happy tidbit of info I was not to discover until checkout time.)

"Here you go, Pro," I said, putting the meat down in front of her.

She sniffed at it dismissively.

I don't do leftovers.

"Oh, for crying out loud, Pro, you'll eat it and like it."

It was about time I laid down the law with that cat.

Ignoring the death ray looks she was shooting me, I headed to the bathroom to wash my face and brush my teeth. After which I grabbed the Holiday Cruise Lines robe in my closet (only $95, should I choose to keep it), threw it on over my *I ♥ My Cat* nightshirt, and headed for the door.

Prozac, who was once more sniffing the roast beef, tried to make me feel guilty with one of her Starving Orphan looks.

If you really hearted your cat, you'd be getting me fresh-baked ham from the buffet bar.

"For once, just do me a favor and cooperate."

And what do you know? After a beat of hesitation, the little devil actually started eating.

Grateful for small miracles, I scooted next door to Cookie's cabin. She came to the door, ashen faced, her eyes rimmed with mascara she hadn't bothered to wash off.

"Cookie, what's going on?"

She ushered me inside and sank down onto her bed.

"Graham's dead," she said, her eyes glazed with disbelief. "Murdered. Stabbed in the heart with an ice pick."

Omigod. So that's what happened to Anton's missing ice picks.

"They found his body early this morning out on the Lido Deck, the ice pick still in his heart. They think I did it. The security guys were here just now searching my cabin for some cuff links the old lady gave him. They think whoever killed him stole the cuff links, too."

Tears began streaming down her cheeks.

"They're going to arrest me, Jaine. I'm sure of it."

"Can they do that without the police?"

She nodded wearily.

"On board ship, the captain makes the laws. They can do anything they want."

"But they don't have any evidence."

"Are you kidding? Three hundred people in the Grand Showroom heard me telling Graham he didn't deserve to live."

"That's not nearly enough to convict you in a court of law."

"But that's not all, Jaine." She took a deep, shuddery breath. "I was at the scene of the crime."

Ouch.

"Graham called me about one in the morning and begged me to meet him out on deck. And like an idiot, I went. He said that hooking up with Emily was the opportunity of a lifetime and that he couldn't afford to pass up the money. He said it wouldn't be long till she kicked the bucket and he inherited her money. After that, he promised, we'd get married. In the meanwhile, he wanted to see me on the side. Can you believe the nerve of that guy? Expecting me to hang around waiting for the poor old biddy to die?"

She got up now and began pacing, angered at the memory.

"At that moment I knew he'd never marry me. He played me for a fool, just like he was playing Emily for a fool. I lost it then and told him what a miserable creep he was. Then I ripped off that stupid pendant he gave me and threw it in his face."

"And they found the pendant when they found his body?"

"With my fingerprints all over it." She nodded glumly. "Not to mention my initials engraved on the damn thing."

I gulped in dismay.

"And it gets worse."

How was that possible?

"They've got an eyewitness who saw me. Eddie Romero, one of the other Gentlemen Escorts.

"Oh, Jaine," she cried, "what am I going to do?"

"I'll help you, Cookie."

"What can you possibly do?" She looked up at me, mascara flowing down her cheeks in tiny rivers.

"I'll investigate."

"Investigate? As in private investigator?"

"I'm not exactly licensed," I confessed, "but I have solved a couple of murders in my time."

(And it's true. I solve murders as a hobby—in between writing assignments and my main job, catering to Prozac's every whim.)

Cookie blinked in amazement.

"Somehow I can't picture you as a private eye."

I get that reaction all the time. A woman in a chenille scrunchy and *I ♥ My Cat* nightshirt doesn't exactly scream Philip Marlowe.

"I'd be happy to help if you'd like," I said.

"That would be wonderful." She managed a feeble smile. "How can I ever thank you?"

"It's the least I can do after all you've done for me," I said, putting my arm around her shoulder. "Just try not to worry. They've done studies that show that ninety-nine percent of the things people worry about never happen. It's a scientific fact."

(No, it wasn't, but I had to say something to get that suicidal look off her face.)

But wouldn't you know, just then, in the Bad Timing Department, there was an ominous banging on the cabin door.

I opened it warily and saw one of the ship's officers, a strapping Scandinavian, looking a bit like old Thor about to let loose with a thunderclap. Flanking him were the same security goons who'd hauled Cookie away last night.

"Cookie Esposito," Thor intoned solemnly, "I'm arresting you for the murder of Graham Palmer."

So much for made-up statistics.

I returned to my cabin, my mind reeling at the thought of Graham stabbed in the heart with an ice pick. I didn't believe for a minute that Cookie was the killer. Why make a big scene in a public place if she intended to bump him off?

I could think of two far more likely suspects at my own dinner table: Kyle Pritchard and Leona Nesbitt. Both had juicy motives to see Graham dead. Kyle, to keep control of Emily's finances. And Nesbitt, to keep her job. Graham had threatened to fire them both. I remembered the murderous look in Nesbitt's eyes at the cocktail party last night, and Kyle's threat to stop Graham from marrying Emily "no matter what it takes."

What if "what it takes" was a stolen ice pick? Kyle said he knew from the get-go that Graham was trouble. What if he swiped Anton's ice picks to nip that trouble in the bud? Then when Emily announced their engagement, Graham's doom was sealed.

Same with Nesbitt. She'd loathed Graham on contact. I could easily picture her hacking her enemy to death and then stopping off at the buffet for a veggie plate.

And what about Robbie? Was he my killer? True, he seemed to like Graham, but that could've been an act. Was it possible he'd knocked off the charming Gentleman Escort to protect his inheritance? My stomach sank at the thought. No, it couldn't be Robbie. I mean, the guy smelled like baby powder.

Shoving the idea of Robbie as a homicidal surf

bum to a dusty corner of my mind, I stepped into the shower and began planning my investigation.

"I need to speak with the captain."

I was at the main desk in the ship's lobby talking to one of the clerks, a deeply tanned dude with dark hair glossed back Armani style. His name tag read Franco.

"Captain Lindstrom is unavailable right now," Franco said, beaming me his official Holiday Handbook employee smile. "Is there anything I can help you with?"

"Nope," I replied firmly. "I need the captain."

"May I ask what it's regarding?"

"Graham Palmer's murder."

"Please keep your voice down," he hissed.

He glanced around to make sure none of the other passengers had heard me, then scurried over to whisper with a puffy blond dame I could only assume was his supervisor. She looked up at me in alarm, then got on her phone.

Minutes later, Franco was escorting me to the captain's office.

"How did you find out about Graham?" he asked as we walked along.

"My cabin's right next door to Cookie Esposito's. I was there when they arrested her."

"You're down on Cookie's deck? That's usually for employees."

"Yes, I'm one of the ship's lecturers."

"Well," he said, all traces of formality gone now that he knew I was a hired hand, "you'd better keep your mouth shut about the murder. It's all very hush-hush. The last thing the Holiday honchos want is a dead body splashed in the news. None of the passengers know except for the old lady he was engaged to. And her family."

"But what about Graham? What are they going to do with his body?"

"They're keeping him in cold storage till we get to L.A."

By now we'd reached Captain Lindstrom's office. But when Franco opened the door to let me in, the captain was nowhere in sight.

"He'll be with you in a minute," Franco said. And then, in a gossipy whisper, he added, "They're having trouble freezing the body."

I stifled a shudder. A little TMI for moi.

Franco trotted off to resume his duties at the front desk, and I took advantage of my alone time to gawk at the captain's impressive digs: Gleaming teak furniture. An entire wall lined with nautical photos. And a scale model of the *Festival* mounted on a stand.

I checked out the model ship, locating the Dungeon Deck mere inches from the bottom, all the while trying not to think of Graham's body decomposing somewhere nearby.

Then I wandered over to Lindstrom's desk, where I saw a framed photo of his family (a smiling wife and four towheaded kids) along with the usual desk accessories.

But what really caught my eye was a plastic bag in his inbox. Inside I could see a wallet, a man's watch—and a half-a-heart pendant with the initials *G.P.* engraved in the center. The same pendant Graham had worn around his neck as a token of his "commitment" to Cookie.

Clearly I'd stumbled upon Graham's personal effects.

I eyed his wallet, dying to snoop inside. Did I dare? Lindstrom could walk in on me any second.

Oh, what the heck. Adrenaline racing, I pulled out the wallet and began rummaging through it.

Graham had the standard collection of credit cards, along with a not-so-standard business card from an establishment called the Hoochie Mama Lounge. When I checked the billfold I was somewhat surprised to find two thousand dollars in cash. Very interesting. Maybe Emily had been showering him with money as well as diamonds.

I was just about to put the wallet away when I noticed a security compartment hidden under the credit cards. I ran my finger inside and felt a piece of paper. Eagerly, I pulled it out. It was a faded newspaper clipping. Just a few paragraphs long— about the arrest of a bank robber known as the Butterfly Bandit, so called because of a large tattoo of a butterfly on his chest.

What was an old crime clipping doing in his wallet? Could Graham have been the Butterfly Bandit? He'd been a lowlife, for sure; was it possible he had a criminal record?

Or was the Butterfly Bandit someone else on board ship? Had Graham found out about this guy's criminal past and cashed in on his discovery with a little blackmail? Maybe all that cash in his wallet wasn't from Emily, but from his blackmail victim.

All very interesting questions, none of which I had time to ponder, because just then I heard voices in the hallway.

I frantically stashed the wallet back in the plastic bag, just milliseconds before Captain Lindstrom came striding into the room.

A rosy-cheeked guy who looked like he'd had one too many Swedish meatballs at the midnight buffet, he spoke with the merest hint of a Scandinavian accent.

"Sorry to have kept you waiting," he said.

"No problem," I replied from the chair I'd hurled myself into.

He settled behind his massive desk and glanced over at the plastic bag.

Oh, Lord. Could he tell I'd tampered with it? Maybe he could see that the objects inside had been moved. I broke out in a cold sweat, wondering if I'd soon be bunkmates with Cookie in the brig. But no, he simply adjusted the picture of his wife and kids and turned his gaze back to me.

"So, Ms. Austen. Apparently you know about Graham's death."

"Yes, my cabin's right next door to Cookie Esposito's. I was there when they arrested her. And I think you're making a grave mistake."

"Oh?" His pale brows lifted in surprise. "Why is that?"

I quickly filled him in on the angry sparks that had flown between Graham and my two leading suspects, Kyle and Ms. Nesbitt.

"Graham threatened to fire them both. Which means they had motives just as strong, if not stronger, than Cookie. You should be searching *their* cabins for the missing cuff links."

He smiled a jolly Santa Claus smile and heaved himself up from his desk.

"Come here, Ms. Austen. Let me show you something."

He led me over to the wall of framed photos, most of them ships in the Holiday arsenal. In several of the pictures, Captain Lindstrom was standing with celebrities. Among others, I saw the good captain with Bill Clinton, Jay Leno, and Paris Hilton (who had inscribed her photo, *To Captain "Lindy"—You're Hot! XOXO, Paris*).

But the captain hadn't brought me there to gawk at celebrities.

There was someone else he wanted me to see.

"Take a look at that one," he said, pointing to a

faded black-and-white picture of a young woman standing on the deck of a ship, a gangly girl in vintage 1950s attire—a shirtwaist dress, locket, and penny loafers.

"That young woman," he said, "is Emily Pritchard."

I took a closer look. Omigosh. It *was* Emily! I could see it in her sweet smile. Standing next to her was an austere older man in a three-piece suit. Probably her father, who'd introduced her to cruising all those years ago.

"Emily has been sailing with Holiday Cruise Lines ever since that picture was taken, more than fifty years ago," the captain said, breaking into my musings. "She's one of our most loyal customers, and I am not about to accuse one of her party of murder."

He crossed his arms over his substantial chest and glared at me, all traces of Santa Claus vanishing up the chimney.

"Is that understood?"

I had been intending to wow him with my credentials as a part-time unlicensed P.I., but somehow I sensed this was not the time.

"Understood." I nodded sheepishly.

He was heading back to his desk when he stopped in his tracks.

"Wait a minute." He turned to peer at me. "Jaine Austen. Aren't you the one who's teaching the memoir-writing class? The one whose students are getting a divorce because of an essay they wrote for you?"

Damn that Paige. She'd ratted me out.

"Yes," I confessed, "but surely you can't blame me for an innocent essay assignment."

Oh, yes, he could.

He proceeded to ream into me with all the cordiality of Simon Legree chatting with an uncooperative plantation hand.

Finally, he wound down his harangue.

"You've done quite enough damage on this cruise, young woman. Until we dock in Los Angeles, I expect you to keep your mouth shut and mind your own business."

Moi? Mind my own business?

The good captain clearly didn't know me very well.

Chapter 11

Ignoring Captain Lindstrom's warning, I set off to have a little chat with Eddie Romero, the eyewitness who saw Cookie fighting with Graham.

Luckily he picked up the phone when I had the ship's operator connect me to his cabin. I told him I had a matter of utmost importance to discuss with him, and minutes later I was trotting over to his digs, not far from mine on the Dungeon Deck.

He came to the door, a low-rent version of Graham.

On the one hand, he was tall and craggy with a thick mane of salt-and-pepper hair. The kind of silver-haired smoothie the ships love to hire to dance with the single ladies. But he had the slightly flattened nose of a street fighter, and when he opened his mouth to talk, it sounded like he'd spent his formative years hanging out with *The Sopranos*.

Right away I wondered if he was the Butterfly Bandit. I could certainly picture him posing for a mug shot.

Looking down, I saw that his feet were bare, his pants rolled up to his calves.

"Excuse my feet," he said, following my gaze. "I'm soaking them."

Like me, he had only one chair in his cabin, and he plopped down into it, easing his feet into a bucket of steaming water.

I perched primly on the only other available seating in the room—his bed—and noticed a much-thumbed issue of *Hustler* on his night-stand.

"What a night I had last night," he moaned. "Got stuck with the world's worst dancer. The woman squashed my toes like a steamroller."

He added some Epsom salts to the water and stirred them with his feet.

"I don't know why I keep wasting my time working these damn cruises. The pay stinks and the cabins are from hunger."

At least you get a spare pillow, I thought, eyeing the two pillows on his bed.

"So what is this matter of utmost importance you want to talk about?" he asked.

"Graham Palmer's murder."

He barely blinked at the mention of Graham's grisly demise.

"Can't say I'm surprised," he said, sloshing his feet around in the water. "It was only a matter of time before some dame popped her cork and let him have it."

"Captain Lindstrom tells me you saw Cookie out on deck with Graham last night."

Notice how I carefully omitted the fact that the captain also told me to mind my own beeswax?

He looked up from his feet, curious.

"What are you, some kind of detective?"

"As a matter of fact, I am," I said, flashing him a badge I'd picked up at a flea market for just such occasions as these. From across the room, he couldn't see that it said *USDA Meat Inspector*.

"Wait a minute." His brow furrowed. "I thought you were a writer. The one whose students are getting a divorce."

For crying out loud, did *everybody* on board ship know about the Shaws' divorce? Was it the front-page headline in the *Holiday Happenings?*

"My writing is just a cover for my detective work," I lied. "A lot of ships like to have a detective on board for situations such as this."

He thought over this whopper and fell for it.

"Very interesting," he said, gazing at me with newfound respect.

"So about Cookie and Graham . . . ?" I prompted.

"I saw them together, all right. I'd just spent two hours hauling Mrs. Two Left Feet around the dance floor, listening to her yap about what a saint her late husband was. The husbands are all saints after they die. It's while they're alive that their wives can't stand them.

"Anyhow, I was sacked out on a deck chair wondering if I'd ever be able to move my toes again when I heard Cookie screaming at Graham. It sounded like it was coming from the deck below, so I looked over the railing, and sure enough, there she was, throwing that half-a-heart pendant in his face."

He took his feet out of the water now and began drying them with one of the ship's threadbare towels.

"What a scam those pendants were. Graham bought 'em by the gross. Gave them out like lollipops at a dentist's office. I'm telling you, the guy had more fiancées than a bridal registry."

He opened a jar of Mineral Ice and began slathering his feet, the sharp aroma of menthol filling the air.

"God, this feels good," he sighed. "Want some?"

He held out the jar.

I shook my head no, opting to stick with my preferred perfume, Eau de Cat Spit.

"What happened after Cookie threw her pendant at Graham?" I asked, getting back to the subject at hand.

"I have no idea. It started to rain, so I went back to my cabin."

"So you didn't actually see Cookie stab Graham?"

"No, but I wouldn't blame her if she did. He treated her like crap."

"Can you think of anybody else he treated badly?"

"Take a number."

"Didn't Graham have *any* friends?"

"No," he said, with a wry smile. "No friends. Just victims."

I couldn't help wondering if Eddie had been one of them.

"You ever hear of the Butterfly Bandit?" I asked.

I watched his reaction closely, looking for signs of guilt or shock. But I saw nada. If he was indeed the Butterfly Bandit, he'd learned how to hide it well.

"Nope," he shrugged. "Can't say I have."

"I found a newspaper clipping about this Butterfly Bandit in Graham's wallet, and I think he might be on board ship. Do you know anyone on the crew who might have had a criminal past?"

He shook his head.

"The only one I can think of is Graham. It wouldn't surprise me if the guy had a record. And it would be just like him to carry a clipping about himself around in his wallet. His fifteen minutes of fame."

I had to admit, he had a point.

"Yeah, what an egomaniac," he said, kneading his toes. "I'm surprised he didn't have the clipping laminated."

Then he picked up a pumice stone and began scraping the dead skin off his calluses.

Definitely my cue to exit.

After leaving Eddie, I strolled around the ship hoping to run into one of the Pritchard clan, but the *Festival* was fairly deserted. We'd docked at Puerto Vallarta that morning, and most of the passengers had already left for shore excursions.

I checked the pool deck and the jogging track and the gift shop—okay, and the buffet, too, where I nabbed myself a banana—but there was not a Pritchard to be found.

So I wandered over to the computer room and read my e-mails, cringing at the thought of my paint-spattered floors. If you ask me, people should be required to get background checks before they're allowed to buy paintbrushes. And by "people," of course, I mean Daddy. Oh, well. I'd just have to cover the mess with an area rug.

Best to forget it and get some work done on Samoa's god-awful manuscript.

Back in my cabin, I found Prozac hard at work clawing my bedspread. Yet another charge to be tacked on to my all-expenses-paid cruise. But it was hard to be angry with her, cooped up as she was in this tiny cabin. She had to do *something* to keep herself amused.

I slumped down in my chair and stared at Samoa's manuscript towering ominously on my night table. I tried to pick it up, but in the end, I simply could not face the thought of another afternoon wrestling with his tortured prose. Not when I was in Puerto Vallarta, one of the world's prettiest resorts.

With a rebellious cry, I leaped up and grabbed my purse and passport.

I'd made up my mind. I was going ashore. True, all the Puerto Vallarta excursions listed in the *Holiday Happenings* were a tad too pricey for me, but I didn't care. I'd hang around the port and at least set foot on Mexican soil. Maybe I could walk over to one of the sandy white beaches and let the ocean lap at my feet.

"See you later, kiddo," I said to Prozac. But she was too engrossed in attacking evil aliens from Planet Bedspread to look up.

Minutes later, I was disembarking the ship. It was a bright sunny day, with no trace of the rain Eddie had seen last night. I skipped down the gangplank with a song in my heart, eager to wiggle my toes in the sand.

The song in my heart gurgled to a halt, however, when I looked around. Where was the beautiful resort I'd seen in the brochures? The one with the sandy beaches and colorful hillside houses?

All I saw now were a few warehouses and some jerry-built jewelry stalls for the gringo touristas. Weaving among those tourists were several local tour guides, touting their excursions.

Okay, so it wasn't paradise. But anything was better than *Do Not Distub*.

I wandered around the jewelry stalls and was gazing at a genuine $29.95 "sapphire" when I was approached by a short, wiry local dressed in Good Humor whites. The only spot of color in his outfit was a bright green parrot perched on his shoulder. A parrot who seemed to be sound asleep. Either that, or dead and stuffed.

"Buenos dias, senorita."

The little Mexican man smiled broadly, exposing a mouthful of what I suspect were store-bought teeth.

"Pepe will show you Puerto Vallarta in a luxury air-conditioned limo. Only fifty American dollars."

"Sorry." I shook my head. No way was I spending fifty bucks to tour Puerto Vallarta with a dead parrot.

I wandered over to another stall, but Pepe was hot on my heels.

"For such a pretty senorita like you," he grinned, "thirty American dollars."

"I don't think so."

"Okay, twenty."

Twenty dollars? That was more like it.

"I show you all the sights. Old Town, Our Lady of Guadalupe Church, a genuine pottery factory, and the most famous cantina in all of Puerto Vallarta."

That sounded pretty good, but I still wasn't sure I wanted to add another twenty bucks to my ever-growing vacation tab. On the other hand, the sun was getting awfully hot, and the thought of a nice air-conditioned limo was pretty darn tempting.

I was standing there considering Pepe's offer when I heard someone screaming:

"You should be ashamed of yourself! Ashamed of yourself!"

What on earth was that all about?

I turned and saw David and Nancy Shaw coming down the gangplank, separated by a gaggle of relatives. Nancy was weeping into a hanky, while David shouted at the top of his lungs, red faced with rage.

To my utter mortification, I realized he was shouting at me.

The next thing I knew he was marching over to where I was standing with Pepe, a Greek chorus of relatives trailing behind him.

"This woman destroyed my marriage!" he

announced to the crowd that was forming around us.

"If it weren't for you," he screamed at me, "I'd be renewing my wedding vows!"

"I'm so sorry, Mr. Shaw, I had no idea—"

"Forty years down the drain because of your stupid essay!"

By now everyone in port was looking at us. Even Pepe's parrot had opened his eyes. So he wasn't dead after all. Just napping.

"What have you got to say for yourself?" David shouted, his furious face mere inches from mine.

There was only one thing to say at a time like this.

My exact words, if I recall, were, "Okay, Pepe. Take me to your limo."

David's curses echoed behind me as I followed Pepe down the pier.

Where the heck was his darn limo, anyway? All I saw were some pickup trucks and an old hearse.

"Here it is!" Pepe said.

My god! He was pointing to the hearse.

It had been converted into a tour bus, the words *Pepe's Puerto Vallarta Excursions* sloppily hand painted on the doors.

"*This* is your limo?"

"A nineteen fifty-nine Cadillac." He grinned, opening the door with a flourish. "I call her Black Beauty."

Black Hole was more like it. I couldn't possibly get into this thing. But then I turned and saw the Shaws, still waiting for what I assumed was their airport transportation. No way was I going back there to face them.

With a sigh, I forked over a twenty-dollar bill and climbed inside the hearse, where I found four rows of threadbare seats lined up behind the driver's compartment.

All of them empty.

It looked like I was the only tourista foolish enough to have signed on for Pepe's tour.

Brushing away a few stray parrot feathers, I took a seat in the last row, trying not to think of the corpses that had ridden in Black Beauty before me.

Meanwhile the sun was beating down on the hearse, and it was about three thousand degrees inside. I was counting the seconds until we got going and Pepe turned on the air-conditioning.

At last he climbed in the driver's seat and turned to give me another store-bought grin.

"You all set?"

"I can't seem to find my seat belt," I replied, searching for one in vain.

"No seat belts," Pepe happily informed me.

Why was I surprised? I was lucky it had wheels.

"Senorita doesn't need a seat belt. Pepe is a very safe driver. Isn't that right, Desi?"

The parrot yawned in reply.

"*Vamanos!*" Pepe was just about to turn the key

in the ignition when there was a knock on the tinted window.

His face lit up in delight.

"Ah!" he cried. "More suckers!"

Okay, so what he really said was, "More passengers."

He jumped out of the car and raced around to the passenger side.

"*Hola, senoritas!*" I heard him saying. "Climb aboard."

Dammit. It was Rita, the Mary Higgins Clark fanatic from my class. I stifled a groan as she and two pals in floral capri pants sets climbed on board and plopped themselves down in the front row.

The minute Rita saw me in the backseat, she began whispering to her friends.

I considered making a break for it, but by then Pepe had jumped back in the car and taken off in a barrage of backfire.

Are we having fun yet? Desi the parrot squawked.

Oh, well. All I could do was sit back and hope for the best. After all, I was going to see Puerto Vallarta. How bad could it be?

I'll tell you how bad: Think Donner Party, with parrot poop.

For one thing, Pepe's "air conditioning" consisted of a battery-operated fan on his dashboard. That, together with the fact that the windows on the hearse opened about an average of three inches, made for mighty toasty motoring. I do not exaggerate when I say I'd been in saunas cooler than Black Beauty.

True to his word, Pepe took us to many of Puerto Vallarta's tourist attractions: Old Town, Our Lady of Guadalupe Church, and the house where Elizabeth Taylor and Richard Burton once lived. What he did not do, however, was stop the hearse and let us get out to see the darn things.

It was like The Travel Channel on fast-forward.

I expected Rita to raise a stink and start yapping about the fabulous, much better excursions she'd taken on previous cruises. But Rita didn't seem to care that we were being shortchanged on our sight-seeing. She was having too much fun gossiping about me. Occasionally snippets of her conversation drifted back to me:

. . . They were supposed to be renewing their vows, and now they're getting a divorce! All because of her!

. . . She calls herself a writer, and she hasn't even published a book.

. . . She has the nerve to compare herself to Mary Higgins Clark!

Wait a minute! I wanted to shout. *You're the one who keeps comparing me to Mary Higgins Clark. Not me!*

But I was too hot to defend myself. I just sat there, watching Puerto Vallarta speed by in a heat-soaked blur, praying for a breeze to make it past my three inches of open window.

As Pepe whizzed past historical landmarks, he gabbed excitedly about the fabulous jewelry shop he was going to take us to.

"It's where all the Hollywood movie stars shop when they're in Puerto Vallarta!" he exclaimed.

Finally, when the temperature in Black Beauty had reached inferno proportions, Pepe parked the hearse in a distinctly seedy part of town.

"Okay, senoritas!" he announced. "Time to go jewelry shopping."

We stepped over a trash-choked gutter onto a street straight out of downtown Beirut. Paint peeled from the small storefronts; security bars adorned the grimy windows.

Pepe led us over to one of the shops, a small stucco structure that had once been painted yellow but was now mottled gray with dirt and water stains. The sign in the window read, *Pepe's Fine Jewelry*.

Pepe opened the door and waved us inside.

An old man was sitting behind the counter, sound asleep, a thin line of drool trickling from his mouth.

"Papa. Wake up!"

The old man came to with a start.

"We have visitors," Pepe announced. "Let us show them our fine merchandise. All handmade by Mexican artisans."

He showed us a bunch of junk that made the stuff at The 99-Cent Store look like Tiffany originals. If Pepe's jewelry was made by Mexican artisans, they were living in China at the time.

Unfortunately, the inside of Pepe's Fine Jewelry was only slightly less stifling than the inside of the hearse, so while Rita and her friends were buying dubious-quality silver I headed outside to breathe in the muggy tropical air.

As I stood there in the blazing sun, my pores gushing like Niagara Falls, I could hear Desi squawking, *Are we having fun yet?*

After what seemed like eternities, the gang emerged from the jewelry shop, and Pepe herded us back into the hearse. He then drove a grand total of two blocks to Puerto Vallarta's "most famous pottery factory"—Pepe's Pottery Barn, where I passed up the "chance of a lifetime" to buy a genuine I Left My Heart in Puerto Vallarta chips 'n' dip plate.

By now Pepe had given up any hope of parting me from my money and was lavishing all his charm on Senorita Rita and her buddies, Senoritas Marilyn and Judy.

"*Vamanos, senoritas!*" he said when they'd bought their share of pottery and were back in the hearse. "Now, off to the most famous cantina in all of Mexico!"

Three guesses what it was called.

Those of you who did *not* guess Pepe's Cantina,

go to the back of the class and put on your dunce caps.

Lord, what a dive. Thank heavens Pepe led us past the seedy bar up front—where final-stage alcoholics were downing shots of paint thinner—out onto a tiny soot-choked patio.

I took a seat at a rickety table with a torn plastic tablecloth. A dying potted palm nearby provided no shade whatsoever.

Naturally, Rita and her gang sat as far away from me as humanly possible.

A sullen teenage waitress with beady eyes and a mighty cleavage informed me there was a five-dollar drink minimum.

Just as I was being served a lukewarm bottle of water, Pepe stepped up to a microphone in a small clearing that served as a stage.

"And now," he announced, "here to entertain you is the world famous Desi, the talking parrot!"

Unfortunately, the parrot was napping at the time of his introduction. Pepe poked him awake and held out a treat.

Desi eyed it without much enthusiasm.

"Come on, Desi," Pepe smiled. "The senoritas are waiting."

Once more he waved the treat in front of the bird.

Finally, Desi let out a giant squawk and said, *Lucy, I'm home!*

Rita bust a gut over that one, slapping her thighs with glee.

Why couldn't she be half as appreciative in my class?

"What else have you got to say, Desi?" Pepe asked the bored bird, waving another treat in front of his face.

Reluctantly, the bird squawked something that sounded like, *You gotta lotta splainin' to do.*

By now Rita and her buddies were practically peeing in their pants. Maybe it was the paint-thinner piña coladas they'd ordered to drink. I'd heard Rita tell the waitress that piña coladas were Mary Higgins Clark's favorite drink.

For the show's grand finale, Pepe accompanied Desi on the conga drums while the bird belted out an earsplitting rendition of "Babalu."

As I sat there, holding my ears, I thought longingly of the ship. It seemed like decades ago that I was safe in its air-conditioned embrace. What had ever possessed me to go ashore? After all, I had a murder to solve. And a manuscript to edit. What was I doing sitting here listening to a parrot sing "Babalu"?

One thing was for certain:

I sure as heck wasn't having fun yet.

Chapter 12

By the time Pepe released us from captivity—I mean, brought us back to the ship—I was starving. I hadn't had a thing to eat since that banana centuries ago.

Back on board, I raced to the buffet, where I practically kissed the ground in gratitude. Then I loaded my tray with a ham and swiss on rye, an extra-jumbo iced tea, and some poached salmon to take back to Prozac. (And, if you must know, just the weensiest piece of chocolate layer cake. Okay, so it wasn't so weensy. And there was ice cream involved. Two scoops. Oh, don't go shaking your head like that. If you ask me, I deserved every single calorie, after what I'd just been through.)

The buffet was fairly empty at that time of the afternoon, and I was able to nab myself a window table, where I instantly dove into my sandwich, washing it down with giant gulps of iced tea. Every once in a while, I rubbed the frosty glass of tea against my forehead. Ahhhh. What a heavenly contrast to the blazing inferno of Black Beauty.

When I finished eating, I sat back and gazed out the window at the mountains of Puerto Vallarta, the prettiest view I'd seen all day.

I was almost tempted to get myself a glass of wine and get a head start on the cocktail hour, but I couldn't linger. It was way past Prozac's snack time and we all know how cranky she gets when her tummy's empty. I reached for her poached salmon and was wrapping it in some napkins when I heard:

"Really, Ms. Austen, I don't think you're supposed to be doing that."

I looked up and saw Ms. Nesbitt standing over me, holding a mug of coffee and a container of nonfat yogurt.

"Doing what?" I asked.

"Taking food to your cabin." She glared down in disapproval at my kitty care package.

"Oh, it's just something to snack on later," I said, carefully omitting the fact that Prozac would be the one doing the snacking.

"Somehow," she said, eyeing my thighs, "you don't seem like the kind of woman who snacks on poached salmon."

Correct me if I'm wrong, but that was a fairly low blow, n'est-ce pas?

"Oh, but I adore poached salmon," I insisted. "Yum! Can't get enough of it. My friends say I'm a salmon-holic."

"Then why didn't you order it when it was on the menu last night?" she asked, oozing skepticism.

"Was it on the menu? Gee, I didn't see it."

"It was there, all right."

And with a final sniff of disapproval, she marched off to another table.

But I wasn't about to let her get away so easily.

157

Lest you forget, Nesbitt was one of my prime suspects, and I intended to question her. So I got a refill on my iced tea and skedaddled over to where she was sitting.

"Mind if I join you?" I asked with a bright smile.

"Well, actually—"

I slid down across from her before she had a chance to voice her objections.

"So what have you and Emily been up to today?" I asked, pretending I hadn't heard about the murder. I didn't dare tell her I was investigating the case. She'd never fall for my USDA Meat Inspector routine. And it would be just like her to rat on me to the captain.

"Ms. Pritchard has been in bed all day," she said stonily.

"She's not ill, I hope."

"Haven't you heard?"

"Heard what?" I asked, still playing the babe in the woods.

"Graham's dead."

"No!"

"Yes," she nodded, quite chipper at the thought. "Stabbed in the heart with an ice pick. They arrested the singer who made a scene in the showroom last night."

"Cookie?" I asked, in mock surprise.

"Yes. Apparently she stole the ice pick from that greasy sculptor fellow. Probably after his demonstration yesterday."

"Omigosh. I suppose you saw her take it."

"Why would I have seen her?"

Time for a little fib.

"I could've sworn I saw you at the display table after the demonstration was over."

I'd meant to surprise her, and I had.

She looked up, startled.

"I was nowhere near that table!" she protested.

Was that a glimmer of guilt I saw in her eyes? Had Nesbitt been the one who took the ice pick? It certainly would have been easy enough. Everyone in the Pritchard clan had been carrying a shopping bag at the demo; they'd all been to the gift shop that morning. It would've been a snap for Nesbitt to slip an ice pick or two into her shopping bag when no one was looking.

I wracked my brain trying to remember if I'd seen her lingering at the demo table. But all I could remember was Anton's smarmy face, blocking my view.

By now Nesbitt had turned away from me and was staring fixedly out the window.

My keen powers of perception told me our little tête-à-tête had come to an end.

"Catch you later," I said, and left her to binge on her nonfat yogurt.

Down on the Dungeon Deck, I spotted Samoa wheeling his linen cart along the corridor.

Believe it or not, I was actually happy to see him.

"Wait up, Samoa!" I called out, trotting to catch up with him.

"Yes, Ms. Austen?" he said, flashing me his deceptively sweet smile.

"I need your help with a little problem."

And at that, his smile went bye-bye.

"I already told you, Ms. Austen, no more pillows."

"It's not that, Samoa."

"What is it then, this problem of yours?"

"I need to break into some cabins."

Yes, it's true. I'd decided to do a little breaking and entering. According to Cookie, Graham's cuff links had been stolen at the time of his death. Of course, it was possible that an opportunistic thief had come along and taken the cuff links from Graham's already dead body. But not likely. Why would a casual thief risk implicating himself in a murder? The way I figured it, whoever had the cuff links was the killer. Hence my decision to go cuff link hunting.

I explained my plan to Samoa, who knew all about Graham's death and Cookie's subsequent arrest. Apparently it was the topic du jour below deck.

"So how about it, Samoa?" I asked. "Can you get me a passkey? And cabin numbers for Kyle Pritchard and Leona Nesbitt?"

He shook his head.

"Samoa could get fired for that."

"Come on, Samoa," I said, appealing to his better nature, praying that he had one. "We can't sit by and let Cookie get arrested for a crime she didn't commit. We have to help her!"

He thought this over for a beat, rubbing his chin.

Then, with all the gravitas of a sultan agreeing to take on another wife, he proclaimed, "Samoa will do it."

"That's wonderful!"

"On one condition," he added.

"What's that?" I asked, with no small degree of trepidation. I knew only too well what a hard bargain Samoa could drive.

"You type my book for me."

Oh, crud. As if editing his miserable manuscript wasn't enough torture, now he wanted me to type the damn thing, too!

No way. Absolutely not. I refused to wear my fingers to stubs typing that piece of crappola. But just as I was about to tell him so, I thought of Cookie sitting in a cold, damp brig.

"Okay," I agreed, with a sigh. "I'll do it."

"Samoa have friend in security." He smiled, no longer the least bit worried about getting fired. "I bring you passkey tonight at midnight. And while I'm there, you show Samoa what you've done on the book so far."

Uh-oh. Thanks to my many distractions, what I'd done on the book so far could be summed in two words: Not much. I'd have to hurry back to my cabin after dinner and cram in some more editing before my midnight deadline.

"Fine," I agreed. "And one more thing. I'll need Robbie Pritchard's cabin number, too."

A mere formality. But I couldn't in all good conscience call myself a part-time unlicensed P.I. without snooping in Robbie's cabin.

Of course, I'd never find the cuff links there.

At least that's what I was telling myself.

Chapter 13

Emily was AWOL at dinner that night, still sequestered in her cabin with Nesbitt.

According to Robbie, she was utterly devastated over Graham's death.

"I've never seen her this unhappy," he said. He'd come to dinner in chinos and a rumpled polo, looking pretty upset himself.

Kyle, on the other hand, was Mr. Joviality.

"Ah, Ms. Austen," he said, when I'd shown up at the table. "How nice to see you."

Alert the media. He was actually talking to me. With a smile, yet.

I almost fainted when he filled my wineglass with pinot noir. Up until that night, I'd had a hard time getting him to pass me the butter.

Throughout dinner he dominated the conversation, cracking jokes and chattering happily about a kayaking excursion in Mazatlan the next day.

"Remember to bring sun block, honey," he told Maggie, gracing her with a rare smile. "You burn so easily."

For once, he wasn't barking at her like a Marine drill sergeant. She smiled back at him in mute, if somewhat puzzled, gratitude.

All the while Robbie sat quietly, his jaw clenched, turning his wineglass around by the stem.

Yet again, I sensed tension in the air. If you ask me, dinner with the Pritchards ought to come with a valium appetizer.

When they cleared away our entrée dishes, Kyle launched into an X-rated joke about Snow White and the Seven Dwarfs in a deli.

With each beat of the joke, I could see Robbie's jaw grow tighter.

Finally, just as Kyle was delivering the punch line, a rather tacky denouement involving Snow White and a pickle, Robbie exploded.

"What the hell is wrong with you, Kyle?"

Kyle's life-of-the-party smile froze on his face.

"How can you sit there telling jokes when Aunt Emily is so unhappy?"

"Oh, please," Kyle said, waving him away like an unwanted waiter. "She'll get over it. Graham was bad news. Anyone could see he was just after her money."

"And you're not?"

Kyle sat up, clearly affronted.

"What's that supposed to mean?"

"Oh, come on, Kyle. All you ever think about is Aunt Em's estimated market value."

Kyle barked out a laugh.

"As if you're not interested in inheriting a bundle someday. At least I'm honest enough to admit it. And I'm sorry that Aunt Emily is unhappy, but better now than later." He shook his head, disgusted. "Such a foolish woman. Buying Graham those diamond cuff links. Do you realize how much those damn things cost? Seven grand! I wasn't about to let her fritter away her estate like that!"

And suddenly an image flashed in my brain—of Kyle leaning over Graham's dead body yanking off the cuff links, unwilling to part with seven thousand dollars' worth of gold and diamonds.

"Emily's always been foolish," Kyle was saying. "Naïve and gullible. When Grandfather was alive he had to watch her like a hawk."

"If Grandfather hadn't been so busy interfering in her life," Robbie snapped, "she might have wound up happy."

"Really, Robbie, must you air the family's dirty laundry in front of strangers?"

This said with a none-too-subtle glance in my direction. Clearly I was the stranger in question.

"Actually, Ms. Austen," he added, "while my aunt is confined to her cabin, I see no need for you to join us at the dinner table."

Hey, wait a minute. What happened to the guy who just five minutes ago was plying me with pinot noir?

"Kyle!" Maggie gasped in dismay. "How can you be so rude?"

"Years of experience," Robbie snapped, throwing down his napkin. "You really are a piece of work, Kyle. Ms. Austen will join us whenever she damn well pleases. And right now I hope she will join me in getting the hell away from you."

Then he got up from the table so abruptly, I was afraid his chair was going to topple over.

"How about it, Jaine?"

In spite of the fact that they were just about to serve lemon tart for dessert, I got up, too.

We Austens do not hang around where we're not wanted. Besides, I don't much care for lemon tart.

"Kyle's such a jerk," Robbie sighed, licking the scotch off a swizzle stick.

He wasn't going to get an argument from me on that one.

We were sitting at the bar in the Tiki Lounge, where Robbie was soothing his angst with Johnny Walker. I'd refrained from ordering one of the lavish umbrella drinks on the menu and stuck with my usual chardonnay.

Out on the dance floor a group of seventysomething ladies from the Lutheran Church of the

Master in St. Cloud, Minnesota, were learning to do the Electric Slide. I knew where they were from because the handsome wannabe actor/emcee in charge of the festivities had been questioning them on his mike and flirting with them shamelessly.

Robbie, however, was oblivious to the action around us; he just stared into his drink, still upset over the scene at dinner.

"What a family, huh?" he said.

"Well, you know Tolstoy's old gag. Happy families are boring. It's the unhappy ones that are interesting."

"You've read Tolstoy?" he asked, looking up from his drink.

"Not really. But I Google him a lot."

That prompted a wan smile.

"Well, if Tolstoy's right, we Pritchards are probably one of the most interesting families you'll ever meet. As you can tell, there's not a lot of love lost between me and Kyle."

I doubted there was a lot of love lost between Kyle and anybody.

"Kyle's always been a cold fish. It's in the genes. He's just like Grandfather."

"I don't mean to pry"—of course I did—"but what did you mean when you said Emily might have been happy if it hadn't been for your grandfather?"

He took a stiff slug of his drink and swiveled on his bar stool to face me.

"Remember that romance I told you about, when Emily was young, the one that broke her heart?"

"I remember."

"The man she fell in love with didn't measure up to Grandfather's standards. He was a crew member on one of her cruises. They were crazy about each other, and Emily was all set to marry him. But Grandfather put his foot down. He wasn't about to have his only daughter hook up with a lowly crewman. He offered her lover money to go away. And the guy took it. He never saw her again."

"Then he couldn't have really loved her."

"Or maybe Grandfather just scared the bejesus out of him. Grandfather was a pretty intimidating guy. All I know is he was the love of her life, and she never met anybody else."

"How sad," I sighed, hoping my shipboard romance would have a happier ending.

"Poor Aunt Em," Robbie said. "She doesn't deserve to have her heart broken twice in a lifetime. Although Kyle's probably right." He stirred his scotch pensively. "Maybe it's all for the best. Graham was a pretty slimy character."

Possibly even a criminal, I thought, remembering the Butterfly Bandit clipping I'd seen in his wallet.

"Frankly," he said, "I'm not sure I blame that singer for bumping him off."

"Oh, but she didn't!"

"What do you mean?"

"Cookie's in the cabin next to mine. Or she was before they carted her off to the brig. I got to know her pretty well, and I don't believe she's a killer."

"If she didn't kill him, then who did?"

"I have no idea. But whoever it was stole one of Anton's ice picks to do it. I don't suppose you noticed anyone hanging around the display table after his demo, did you?"

"No. After Anton cornered you, I left."

By now the Lutheran ladies had kicked off their orthopedic sneakers and were Electric Sliding on the dance floor with abandon. One of them had grabbed a whistle from around the emcee's neck and was tooting every time his tush came into view, provoking lusty whoops from the rest of the gals.

"At least somebody's having fun on this cruise," Robbie said, noticing them for the first time.

"Probably a little too much fun," I replied as the emcee struggled to get his whistle back.

"By the way," he said, "in all the fuss over the murder, I almost forgot—I've got some good news!"

"Really? What is it?"

He smiled proudly.

"Well, seeing how much you like water sports, I pulled some strings and got you a spot on our scuba excursion the day after tomorrow."

"Scuba diving?" I gulped. "The day after tomorrow?"

"Yes. Isn't that terrific?"

Oh, Lord. Why on earth had I told that outrageous lie? I knew absolutely zippo about scuba diving. And the last thing I wanted was to appear in public in a bathing suit. I was simply going to have to fess up and tell Robbie that the closest I'd ever come to a scuba dive was watching old *Sea Hunt* reruns.

"To be perfectly honest, Robbie, I'm not a very experienced diver."

"As long as you know the basics, you'll be okay. You do know the basics, don't you?"

"Oh, sure, I know the basics."

What was wrong with me? Could I not tell the truth for two consecutive minutes?

"And I promise I'll watch out for you," he assured me. "So how about it? Is it a date?"

He shot me a grin that could melt mozzarella.

"It's a date," I said, caving like you knew I would.

At which point the Lutheran ladies broke out into a deafening chorus of "Save a Horse (Ride a Cowboy)," lassoing the emcee with his microphone cord. Poor guy looked like a rabbit caught in a trap. I knew exactly how he felt.

"What do you say we get out of here and go for a walk on deck?" Robbie asked.

"Gee, I'd love to, but I'm afraid I've got a bit of a headache."

Which was no lie. Thanks to that scuba excursion looming on the horizon, all thoughts of romance had gone flying out the porthole. Besides, I had to get back to the cabin and get some work done on *Do Not Distub* before Samoa showed up for our midnight meeting.

"Oh." Robbie's smile faded.

"Maybe some other night?" I asked.

"Sure," he said, waving to the bartender for another drink.

"Well, see ya."

I slid off my barstool and made my way back to my cabin, wondering how I could possibly lose fifteen pounds in forty-eight hours.

By the time midnight rolled around, I'd managed to plow through half of *Do Not Distub*. I was bleary-eyed with fatigue when Samoa showed up, as promised, with the passkey and requested cabin numbers.

"You must return passkey to Samoa tomorrow afternoon by three o'clock," he commanded, handing it to me.

"Absolutely," I promised. I planned to get started snooping as soon as the Pritchards left for their kayaking excursion. Which, according to the *Holiday Happenings*, began at 9 A.M. So I'd have plenty of time to poke around.

"Now it's time to show Samoa what you've done," he said, making himself at home in my one and only chair.

"Here you go," I said, handing him my sweated-over pages.

He began reading, moving his lips as he did so. Not a good sign. As a rule, lip movers are rarely speed readers. At this rate, we'd be here for hours.

And, alas, we were. He didn't finish until after 2 A.M.

Prozac had a lovely nap during the interim, and I must confess I dozed off a bit myself.

Finally he'd lip-read his last syllable.

"Samoa is finished," he announced, crossing his arms over his chest, very Yul Brynner in *The King and I.*

"Well?" I asked. "What do you think?"

He broke out in a wide grin.

"Samoa is pleased!"

Thank heavens; otherwise there might have been another murder on board.

"*Do Not Distub* will be international best-seller!" he proclaimed.

At which point I could have sworn Prozac rolled her eyes.

Whatever he's smoking, I want some.

"Samoa will go now," he said, getting up from his chair.

I loved the way this guy narrated his own life.

After making me promise once more to return the passkey by three the next afternoon, he finally trotted off.

It had grown pretty stuffy in the cabin, so after he

left I decided to go to the pool deck for some fresh air.

I don't suppose you fell for that, did you? Of course I didn't go to the pool deck for fresh air. I went to the buffet for a brownie. Yes, I know I'm a disgrace—just a few paragraphs ago I was talking about losing fifteen pounds in forty-eight hours— but what can I say? I was hungry!

And it was all that darn Pepe's fault. I'd eaten lunch so late, I'd hardly touched my dinner. And now at 2:30 in the morning I was starving. I'd just have one measly brownie to tide me over till breakfast, at which point I would start a spartan exercise and weight-loss regime.

So don't give me any flak, okay? I get enough of that from my scale.

And besides, I'm only telling you about my shameful caloric lapse because of what happened on my way back from the buffet.

There I was, strolling past the casino, wondering who the genius was who first mixed nuts with chocolate, when I saw a familiar face at the roulette wheel.

It was Kyle's wife, Maggie. What was she doing in the casino in the middle of the night? I looked around for Kyle, but he was nowhere in sight.

Maggie was shaking a pair of dice with surprising expertise, the players around her shouting words of encouragement. Then she tossed them, and a collective groan arose from the table.

Maggie blanched in dismay as her chips were raked away. For a minute, I thought she might even cry.

From the way she'd handled those dice, I could tell Maggie was no casual gambler. Far from it. This gal had "addict" written all over her. With her ashen face, frizzled hair, and gleam of manic desperation in her eyes, she looked like a poster girl for Gamblers Anonymous.

Very interesting.

Up to now Maggie hadn't been on my suspect list, but suddenly I wondered. Could she possibly be the killer? What if she depended on Emily's money to feed her habit? Hadn't Graham threatened to cut off all Kyle's access to Emily's portfolio? Had Maggie stabbed him with Anton's ice pick to keep herself in chips?

Just something to ponder while I ate my brownie.

YOU'VE GOT MAIL

To: Jaineausten
From: Shoptillyoudrop
Subject: Such Wonderful News!

Jaine, sweetheart, why didn't you tell me that you and Lance were engaged??

To: Jaineausten
From: DaddyO
Subject: Congratulations, Lambchop!

Your mom just told me the good news!

Lance seems like a very nice fellow. Of course, in my eyes, no fella's good enough for my lambchop. But if he makes you happy, that's all that counts!

Love and kisses,

Daddy (aka The Father of the Bride)

To: Jaineausten
From: Sir Lancelot
Subject: Don't Kill Me

Don't kill me, Jaine, but I told your mom that you and I were engaged. I was helping her do the dishes after dinner, and she started talking about how I needed a special gal in my life. I told her I already had a special gal in my life—you—and somehow she just assumed we were boyfriend and girlfriend. I wanted to tell her the truth, but she was so happy, I couldn't bust her bubble.

Anyhow one thing led to another and the next thing I knew I'd invented this fabulous love affair culminating when I proposed to you on bended knees after a moonlit stroll on the beach. The bottom line is—after I get off work this afternoon, we're going to check out wedding chapels.

But don't worry. I promise I'll tell her the truth today.

Love from,

Lance

To: Jaineausten
From: Shoptillyoudrop
Subject: I Almost Forgot

Jaine, honey—

In all the excitement of the wedding, I almost forgot: I hired a handyman to get the paint stains off your floor. A very nice fellow named Ricardo. I saw him doing some work for one of your neighbors up the street, and as luck would have it, he said he'd be free today to stop by. And he's only charging $30! What a bargain!

Daddy agrees it's best we let a professional take over from here. He's going to stay home and "supervise" while Lance and I look at wedding venues.

Oops. There's Lance at the door now.

More later!

XXX,

Mom

To: Jaineausten
From: DaddyO
Subject: Outraged!

Would you believe your mother hired a handyman to clean a few drops of paint from the floor?

If your mom thinks I'm going to pay some stranger off the streets thirty bucks for a job I can do blindfolded, she's nuts!

Love and kisses from your outraged,

Daddy

To: Jaineausten
From: Shoptillyoudrop
Subject: A Beachside Wedding!

Jaine, darling, I just this minute got back from looking at wedding venues and had to race to the computer to tell you all about it. We've found the ideal spot! A lovely hotel right on the beach! Just think! A beachside wedding. How utterly romantic!

Of course, it's terribly expensive but Lance really seemed to hit it off with the hotel manager, and I'm hoping we'll be able to get a discount. Afterward Lance and I had cocktails out on the hotel's terrace. Oh, honey. I had a whiskey sour and it went straight to my head!

Lance has such wonderful ideas for the wedding. He's so creative. Unlike your father, who wants to have the wedding at the Tampa Vistas clubhouse, and serve chili cheese dogs at the reception. My goodness, have you ever heard of anything so silly?

Well, time to get dinner started. Not that I'm the least bit hungry. That sweet hotel manager sent us complimentary hors d'oeuvres with our cocktails.

Love from,

Mom

To: Jaineausten
From: Sir Lancelot
Subject: Fabulous News!

Fabulous news, Jaine! I met the most wonderful guy, the manager at the Casa Del Mar Hotel. What a dreamboat. I swear, he could be Mr. Right. Anyhow, I never did get around to telling your mom the truth about our "engagement." She was having so much fun, it just didn't seem like the right time. But I swear I'll tell her tomorrow when we go to check out wedding cakes.

Signing off from cloud nine, your fiancé (ha-ha!),

Lance

To: Jaineausten
From: Shoptillyoudrop
Subject: So Mad I Could Spit!

Something simply awful has happened!

I was on my way to the kitchen to fix dinner when I looked down and saw the most horrible mess on the living room floor!

You're not going to believe this, but Daddy sent Ricardo away this afternoon and tried to clean up the paint stains himself. He got out the stains, all right, but the darn fool wound up taking up the walnut finish. So now, instead of a few drops of paint on your floor, you've got a big white patch of bare wood!

I am so mad at your father I could just spit!

Your disgusted,

Mom

To: Jaineausten
From: DaddyO
Subject: Minor Mishap

Good news, honey! I got all the paint off your

floor. One tiny problem, though. Some of the finish came off, too. But fear not. I'll just pick up some walnut stain at the hardware store, and your floor will be as good as new! Easy-sneezy, no problemo!

Love and kisses,

Daddy

PS. Don't worry about hiring a musician for the wedding, lambchop. I'll be happy to play my accordion.

Chapter 14

The next morning Prozac clawed me awake for her breakfast at the ghastly hour of seven A.M.

Let's do the math, shall we? Asleep at three, awake at seven. That's four not-so-refreshing hours of sleep.

"Prozac, show a little mercy," I groaned.

But she went right on to digging her claws into my chest.

With a weary sigh, I dragged myself out of bed and tossed her some roast turkey I'd picked up on my brownie run last night.

She turned up her little pink nose in disgust. I knew what she was thinking.

Leftovers again?

"It's not leftovers; it's barely four hours old!"

Seeing that I wasn't about to dash over to the buffet for a replacement breakfast, she reluctantly started eating.

The minute she did, I scrambled back into bed, hoping to get some more sleep. But as much as I tried, sleep would not come. I just laid there, listening to the snorting noise Prozac makes when she inhales her food. Out in the hallway, early birds were clomping past my room to start their day, their footsteps echoing like cannons.

It looked like I was up for good.

So once more I pried myself out of bed. Then,

true to my vow to whittle away some unwanted pounds before Scuba Day, I threw on some sweats and headed off to the jogging track.

High up on the prow of the ship, the jogging track provided an unsurpassed view of the ocean. But what really caught my eye was the sight of Kyle and Maggie doing laps.

Good heavens. Weren't they about to head off to Mazatlan for a day of strenuous kayaking? And yet there they were, working out before a workout. Talk about gluttons for punishment.

Clad in shorts and a sweatshirt, his muscular legs churning like pistons, Kyle whizzed along with impressive speed. Maggie—like me, a charter member of the cellulite club—struggled to keep up with him. After a grueling night at the casino, the bags under her eyes were the size of carry-ons.

I waved to her, but, lost in her thoughts, she didn't see me. Kyle saw me but chose to ignore me.

I took a deep breath and stepped out onto the track. There was no delaying it any longer. Time to burn some calories.

I managed to keep up a nice steady trot for all of about thirty seconds. After which, my heart pounding in protest, I settled for a fast walk.

It was then that I heard Kyle and Maggie coming up behind me.

"Oh, Kyle," Maggie was saying, "I'm worried. "What if the police find out?"

The police? Find out what?

I was hoping to hear more tidbits as they overtook me on their laps, but before I knew it, Kyle had Maggie by the elbow and was hustling her off the track, shooting me a nervous glance as they left.

I continued to puff along, my brain in overdrive. What exactly was it that Maggie was afraid the cops would find out? That Maggie was the killer? Or that Kyle had done the dirty deed? Or who knew? Maybe they did it together. The family that slays together stays together and all that.

Whatever it was, I intended to find out.

Puffing around the track for the next forty minutes, I worked up quite an appetite. That's the trouble with exercising: Aside from the sheer agony of it, it makes you so darn hungry.

By the time I staggered over to the buffet, I was ready to eat the wallpaper.

I'd meant to have a microscopic breakfast of dry toast and coffee, but when I saw a mountain of fluffy scrambled eggs fresh from the frying pan, I couldn't resist taking just a tiny bit. And why not throw a pat of butter on my toast? How many calories could that possibly be?

Fifteen minutes later, I'd scarfed down two pieces of toast. With butter and jam. Not to mention a side of bacon with my scrambled eggs.

Oh, well. I needed my strength for my day of breaking and entering. And the more I thought about it, the whole idea of going on a diet on a cruise was absurd. What woman in her right mind tries to lose weight with a twenty-four-hour buffet just a hop, skip, and a deck away? Certainly not moi.

Besides, there was no need to lose fifteen pounds before that scuba excursion. I simply wouldn't go. After all, I was a writer. A creative person. Surely, I could come up with some clever excuse to get out of it.

In the meanwhile, I helped myself to some more bacon.

By now you'd think I would've learned to Just Say No to e-mails. But much like a dental patient who can't help probing a sore tooth, I felt myself helplessly drawn to the computer room.

Can you believe Lance—telling my parents we were engaged? And what about my parents? Did they have no gaydar whatsoever? I swear, those two wouldn't recognize a gay man at a Broadway opening.

I came *thisclose* to calling Lance ship-to-shore and reading him the riot act. But that would have undoubtedly added another zillion dollars to my ever-growing tab, so instead I did the sensible thing:

I returned to my cabin to get ready for a day of breaking and entering.

After a quick shower, I slipped into some elastic-waist jeans and a T-shirt and secured my curls in a scrunchy. Then I retrieved the treasured passkey from my room safe, where I'd stowed it.

I was just about to head out the door when it hit me: The room safe! All the cabins had them. Chances are, whoever took Graham's cuff links had stowed them in his or her room safe.

I sank down on my bed with a sigh. What good was the passkey if I couldn't get into the safes?

Now what was I going to do?

Once again I had to turn to Samoa for help. I figured his friend in security would know how to open the safes. They were simple boxes operated via a numeric keypad. Every time you used the safe, you programmed in a four-digit code number. Surely there had to be a universal override code.

I just prayed Samoa's buddy would have access to it.

I found Samoa in one of the cabins down the corridor and raced in, breathless.

"Samoa, you've got to help me!"

Heaven only knew what he'd demand as payment this time. Probably my firstborn.

He looked up from where he was making the beds.

"People are such pigs," he said, plucking a pretzel from the sheets.

"Look, Samoa," I said, grateful he'd never seen the Ben & Jerry carton lids I've been known to wake up with. "That friend of yours in security. Does he know the override code to the room safes?"

"Sure."

Hallelujah!

"Can you get it for me?"

"Are you crazy?" He plucked a banana peel from the tangled mass of sheets. "Too dangerous. Samoa could get fired for that."

"But, Samoa, it's important!"

"Sorry. Until Samoa is best-selling author, he can't afford to lose his job on ship."

I begged and pleaded, but to no avail. He went on making the bed, cursing the slovenly habits of his charges. Frankly, I don't think he was the least bit scared of losing his job. I think he just ran out of things to bribe me for.

I trudged back to my cabin, momentarily defeated.

But only momentarily.

Once more, the Austen can-do spirit rose to the occasion.

There had to be another way to crack the safes.

I hunkered down and put the old noggin to work. And after several minutes of asking myself WWSD (What Would Sherlock Do?), I came up with Operation Override.

A half hour later, a security guy was at my cabin door.

Like Samoa, he was dark and slight. Maybe they

came from the same mysterious country. According to the tag on his work shirt, his name was Lolong.

"Come on in," I said, ushering him past the bathroom, where Prozac was stashed with a mini-mountain of poached salmon. The salmon would keep her quiet for a few minutes, which is all the time Operation Override would require.

"Silly me," I said, playing the helpless lady in distress. "I forgot the code number on my safe."

"Not a problem," Lolong said, in an accent much like Samoa's.

"I was sort of tipsy when I punched it in last night. Too many mai tais at the Tiki Lounge. Ha-ha."

"Not a problem," he repeated. "Happens all the time."

And here's where my brilliant plan came into play. Clearly Lolong would have to use the override code to open my safe. All I had to do was watch and see what numbers he punched in.

Of course, things didn't go quite that smoothly. Lolong hovered over the safe, trying to block my view.

But he didn't realize who he was up against.

I, Jaine Austen, happen to be an ace snoop. Reading over my neighbor's shoulder is a skill I perfected years ago on crowded airplanes. I've been known to read entire novels without ever turning a page.

So it was easy-sneezy, as Daddy would say, to peek over Lolong's shoulder and read the override numbers as he punched them in.

Of course, it didn't hurt that he was five feet three inches, tops.

The code was 89326. Immediately I came up with a mnemonic device to help me remember it. An 89-year-old marries a 32-year-old and they have 6 children. 89326.

"All done, miss." Lolong gestured to the open safe door, where I'd stashed some cheap costume jewelry.

"Thank you so much!"

"Not a problem. And next time, go easy on the mai tais."

"Oh, I will, Lolong! I will!"

I followed him to the door, feeling enormously proud of myself. Really, one of these days I had to get myself a P.I. license. I just hoped they gave them to people who're afraid of guns.

Then, just as I was patting myself on the back for a job superlatively done, a plaintive wail erupted from the bathroom.

Darn that Prozac. She must've finished her salmon.

Lolong stopped in his tracks.

"What was that?"

"Oh, the plumbing's been making strange noises all morning," I said, putting on my tap shoes.

He reached for a walkie-talkie hanging from his belt.

"I'll get the plumbers here right away."

"No!" I screeched. "I mean, don't bother. I already called. They should be here any minute. Honest, it's not a problem," I added, hoping he'd be convinced by his own mantra.

"Okay, then," he nodded, "I guess I'll be going." And at last he headed off down the corridor.

Limp with relief, I raced over to the Holiday notepad on my night table and wrote down the override code.

Then I let Prozac out of the bathroom.

She shot me one of her patented *How could you?* looks and shuffled across the carpet like she'd just done a seven-year stretch in Siberia.

Lord knows there'd be hell to pay. She'd punish me for this somehow.

But I'd worry about that later.

Right now, I had some breaking and entering to do.

Chapter 15

Armed with the override code and the cabin numbers Samoa had given me, I set out on my investigation.

I figured I'd start with my Number One Suspect—Kyle Pritchard.

I found his cabin easily enough. But as bad luck would have it, just as I was about to let myself in, a silver-haired couple came out from the room across the way. Oh, phooey. What if they'd gotten friendly with Kyle and Maggie? What if they put two and two together and figured out I was neither Kyle nor Maggie?

Then I realized that the top I'd thrown on in my haste to get dressed was my *Cuckoo for Cocoa Puffs* T-shirt. Why on earth had I chosen something so tacky to wear here on the high-rent Capri Deck? It practically screamed interloper.

"Hi, there," I said, trotting out my most confident *I-belong-here* smile.

Inwardly I cringed, waiting for suspicious stares and muttered responses, but those darling people smiled broadly and returned my hello.

"Oh, we love Cocoa Puffs, too!" said the woman, in a molasses-thick Southern accent.

"Y'all have a nice day," her husband chimed in as they started down the corridor.

What a relief. I should've known Kyle wasn't the type to make friends.

Alone at last, I let myself in with the passkey and entered the promised land.

Although not as grand as Emily's palatial suite, Kyle and Maggie's cabin, with its roomy sitting area and sweeping balcony, was pretty darn swellegant. And thank heavens it had already been cleaned. At least I wouldn't have to worry about their steward busting in on me.

Getting down to business, I made a beeline for the safe and punched in the override code.

Voila, it worked!

I blinked at the sight of the bling inside: a diamond brooch, a honker citrine ring, and a Rolex watch that cost more than my Corolla. If this stuff was real—and I had no reason to doubt it wasn't—it looked like Kyle and Maggie had a high standard of spending to maintain.

I rooted around among the baubles, but alas, there were no diamond-studded cuff links.

Fighting back my disappointment, I proceeded to search the rest of the cabin, rifling through drawers, under the mattress, between sofa cushions, and in the mini-fridge—where I came *this-close* to nipping their macadamia nuts.

When all was said and done, I came up with nothing more interesting than a bottle of Grecian Formula and enough Ralph Lauren polos to open a boutique in Bloomie's.

Finally, I had to admit that Kyle's cabin was cuff link-free.

So I set out to investigate my second-favorite Person I'd Most Like to See Behind Bars—Leona Nesbitt.

I was just about to barge into Nesbitt's cabin when it occurred to me that she could be inside. I doubted she and Emily had gone off kayaking, not with Emily so unhappy.

So I knocked tentatively. If Nesbitt answered the door, I'd just tell her I was worried about Emily and wanted to find out how she was doing. But, fortunately, there was no answer, so I let myself in with my handy-dandy passkey and hustled over to her safe.

Alas, it yielded nothing of interest. Just a passport and a string of pearls.

Nosy parker that I am, I couldn't resist taking a peek at her passport photo. Now I know nobody looks good in a passport photo, but this one made mine look like a *Cosmo* cover. Nesbitt glared into the camera, her mouth set in a grim line of disapproval, clearly annoyed at the U.S. government for making her sit through this folderol.

Next I checked out her closet, where her Easy Spirits were lined up like a row of orthopedic soldiers. I rummaged through her clothing, marveling at how one woman could own so many puke-green outfits.

It's when I started searching through her shoes (always a good hiding place) that I was in for a surprise. Stowed away in the back of the closet was a pair of five-inch wedgie stilettos, the kind seen in strip joints and on questionable street corners.

Hello. What was the battle-axe doing with hooker wedgies?

Things got even steamier when I opened her lingerie drawer. There, among her bunion pads and support hose, was a treasure trove of underwear that would make a Victoria's Secret model blush:

lacy bras and thong undies and X-rated teddies with cutouts in strategic places. Not to mention a jar of edible body chocolate.

For a minute I wondered if I'd let myself into the wrong cabin.

I was in the right place, all right. A fact that was about to be verified with startling clarity. Because just as I was busy examining a leopard-skin thong, the door started to open.

Frantic, I looked around for somewhere to hide. The only place possible was the closet. I'd just managed to jam myself in among her Easy Spirits when Nesbitt came into the room.

And apparently she was not alone.

"Oh, darling!" I heard her gush. "I've missed you so!"

Darling? Who the heck was she calling darling?

"Me, too, sweetheart," a familiar voice replied.

Omigosh. It was Kyle! What was he doing here? He was supposed to be kayaking.

I guess Nesbitt was wondering the same thing.

"How did you ever manage to get away?" she asked.

"Easy," Kyle said. "I faked a migraine on the tour bus."

"How clever of you," Nesbitt cooed, her voice all soft and gooey.

"It sure was, sweetcakes. Now put on something sexy for your studmuffin so we can have some fun."

Sweetcakes? Studmuffin? What alternative universe had I wandered into?

"And don't forget your high heels. You know how they turn me on."

High heels? Lord, no! I stared at the hooker wedgies in the corner of the closet. Any second now, Nesbitt would open the closet door and see me. I'd be hauled off to the brig so fast my head would be spinning.

But then I heard eight little words that brought joy to my heart:

"Not today, hon," Nesbitt said. "My bunions are killing me."

"Oh, all right," Kyle pouted. "Just bring the body chocolate."

Nesbitt proceeded to don "something sexy" and the next thing I knew mattress springs were squeaking, body chocolate was squishing, and the two of them were moaning in ecstasy.

Holy Moses. The stuffy investment banker was having an affair with the uptight companion. Neither of whom was the least bit stuffy or uptight now.

This is a family novel so I'll spare you the details of their sexcapades, but let's just say they started out with a game called *Willy's Wonka and the Chocolate Factory*, a nauseating caper the sounds of which haunt me to this day.

I spent the entire afternoon trapped in that awful closet, squatting on a pair of sweaty sneakers whose Odor-Eaters definitely needed replacement.

Finally, having exhausted themselves (and the mattress springs), the lovebirds fell silent. One of them began to snore. I was betting it was Nesbitt. I opened the closet door and peeked out; sure enough, they were both sound asleep, Nesbitt snoring like a stevedore.

And I took advantage of this lull in the action to get my sweetcakes the heck out of there.

It wasn't until I was in the elevator on my way down to the Dungeon Deck that I began to think about Ms. Nesbitt's sweaty sneakers. I remembered what Eddie Romero said about how it had rained the night of the murder. That's why he got up and went back inside.

And then it hit me. Maybe it wasn't sweat I'd felt under my tush all afternoon. Maybe it was rainwater. Maybe Nesbitt's sneakers got wet while she was out on deck in the rain sticking an ice pick in Graham Palmer's heart.

Chapter 16

Samoa is very distub."
I found my not-so-genial steward waiting for me when I limped back to my cabin, his arms plastered across his chest, still doing Yul Brynner in *The King and I*.

For a little guy he was pretty darn intimidating.

"You were supposed to be back at three

o'clock. It's now five. Samoa waiting three hours."

Looked like his math skills were as stinky as his English.

"I'm so sorry, Samoa, but I got unavoidably detained."

Best not to go into details about my afternoon hiding out in Nesbitt's closet. Something told me he would not want to hear how close I came to getting busted with an illegally obtained passkey.

"Samoa very distub," he repeated, snatching the passkey from my hand.

"I don't suppose I can borrow it again?" I asked, with a hopeful smile.

He didn't even bother to answer that one, just strode out the door muttering something unintelligible about a note he'd left me.

"You should probably check the mattress in Leona Nesbitt's cabin," I called after him. "I think the springs might be broken."

Then I shut the door and turned to Prozac.

"You wouldn't believe the ghastly afternoon I just had. I got trapped in a ridiculously tiny closet, forced to listen to sexual acrobatics that would make Masters and Johnson blush. It was hell, I tell you. Hell with smelly sneakers!"

But if it was sympathy I was after, I was barking up the wrong kitty.

She glared up at me from her perch on my pillow.

Do you realize how long it's been since my last snack?

Then she jumped down and began doing her patented Feed Me dance around my ankles.

With a sigh, I trudged down to the buffet to load up on poached salmon.

"You really like salmon, huh?" the guy behind the counter asked as I helped myself to a chunk. This was only about the seventeenth time I'd gotten it.

"Love the stuff. It's packed with vitamins and essential omega beta carotene fish oils," I blathered, making up nutrients as I went along.

Back in the cabin, I gave Prozac her food and dragged myself to the bathroom, yearning to soak my weary limbs in a nice relaxing bubble bath. Seeing as I had no tub, however, it looked like I was going to have to settle for a tepid phone booth–sized shower.

And even that was not to be. Because the first thing I saw when I stepped into my bathroom was that note Samoa had mentioned, propped up on the vanity counter:

Samoa axidental spil liter box. Nut wury.
All klene now.

For those of you not fluent in Samoan (by now I was an expert), that meant:

Samoa accidentally spilled the litter box.
Not to worry. All clean now.

I looked over at the litter box and groaned. Samoa had cleaned the litter box, all right. The darn fool had carted away all but about five grains of sand. Unless Prozac's bladder had shrunk to the size of a thimble, it looked like I was going to have to raid the kiddie sandbox.

For a minute I considered waiting until after dinner, but I couldn't risk it. There was no telling where Prozac might poop, and I was not about to add a "new carpeting" charge to my ever-growing bill.

So I threw on the clothes I'd just thrown off and headed out in search of the sandbox. I found it on the pool deck in the rear of the ship. By now it was almost six and I figured it would be deserted.

I figured wrong. There, plopped in the center of the sand, was a towheaded toddler, building what was either a castle or a giant boob.

Oh, for crying out loud. What was he doing here at this hour? Shouldn't he be in bed? Or at least having his dinner?

A woman I assumed was his mother was stretched out on a nearby chaise, dozing. And thank heavens she was the only other adult around. I'd be able to sand-nap without any witnesses.

I approached the sandbox with a sappy smile on my face.

"Hello, little boy."

Having no children of my own, I haven't quite mastered the art of conversing with little ones.

"Kitty cat!" he gurgled in reply.

Omigosh. It was the same kid who'd spotted Prozac on line at the pier.

"Kitty cat!" he gurgled, louder this time, a big grin on his face, clearly thrilled to see me again.

The feeling, I regret to say, was not mutual.

"Keep it down, will ya?" I begged, shooting an anxious glance at his mother, who luckily had not woken up.

But the kid was on a roll. "Kitty cat," he said again, his idea of sparkling repartee.

Somehow I had to shut him up.

"Here," I said, handing him an oatmeal raisin cookie I just happened to find on the ledge of the sandbox. (Okay, so I didn't just happen to find it. I picked it up at the buffet on my salmon run. Are you happy now?)

The kid grabbed it eagerly and began munching.

At last, blessed silence. I took out the Holiday Cruise Lines laundry bag I'd brought along for my heist and hurriedly began scooping sand into it.

All was going smoothly. The kid was munching. I was scooping. And soon Prozac would be pooping in fresh sand.

Then, just as I was scooping out my last fistful of sand, tragedy struck.

A San Andreas–type chasm suddenly appeared in the sand. I watched, transfixed, as it quickly snaked its way to the kid's boob/castle.

Before I knew it, the boob/castle was crumbling apart. And the kid was bawling at the top of his lungs.

"Cassul bwoke! Cassul bwoke!"

So it was a castle and not a boob. At least one mystery on this ship was solved.

The next thing I knew the kid's mom sprang awake and was racing over to the sandbox.

"What's going on here?" she cried, scooping him up in her arms.

"Cassul bwoke," he whimpered, tears streaming down his face.

"I'm so sorry. It was an accident," I piped up. "I was just getting some sand, and out of nowhere the sand shifted and—"

"What on earth are you eating, Devon?"

Momentarily forgetting the castle fiasco, his mother turned her attention to the remains of a rather sandy oatmeal raisin cookie.

"I gave him a cookie."

"You gave him a *cookie?*"

She glared at me as if I'd just fed him rat poison.

"Why on earth did you do that? Devon doesn't eat refined sugar."

Yeah, right. Eighteen years from now Devon will be sitting in a college dorm stuffing his face with Sara Lee.

"And besides, I just gave him some all-natural gum-free gummy bears a half hour ago."

"Gee, I didn't realize—"

"And what, may I ask, are you doing putting sand in a laundry bag?"

This last question did not come from Devon's mom—but from Paige.

Yes, that's right. Like an unwelcome ghost, my jolly social director had materialized out of nowhere, clipboard akimbo.

"Well?" she asked. "What are you doing with the sand?"

Oh, Lord. What was I going to tell her?

After a few agonized beats, I came up with an explanation. A rather clever one, if I do say so myself.

"I need it for my class."

"Why in the world would you need sand for your class?"

"I'm going to have my students describe it. It's a very popular writing exercise. They teach it at all the universities."

Pretty good for a spur-of-the-moment whopper, huh?

Then, with all the dignity a woman with a laundry bag of sand can muster, I got up and stalked off.

Which would've been pretty darn dignified, too, if it hadn't been for that all-natural gum-free gummy bear stuck to my fanny.

By now I was a walking zombie. You'd be, too, if you'd just spent a day breaking into cabins and getting trapped in a closet, listening to sexual antics that would make a porn star blush. Not to mention masterminding a daring sandbox kitty litter heist.

I trudged back to my cabin with my sack of sand, longing to hit the pillow, if only I had one. After tossing the sand in Prozac's makeshift litter box, I collapsed onto my bed and set my alarm in time to get up for dinner.

I managed to grab a refreshing twelve minutes of sleep before it blared me awake.

Then I showered and dressed in record speed and dashed to the dining room, where I found Emily and Ms. Nesbitt back in their seats.

Emily greeted me with a faint smile, her face wan, her permed curls limp, all traces of her former ebullient self vanished.

Kyle was all over her, playing the part of the loving nephew, pretending to be concerned over "her loss." As if he hadn't practically broken out in a jig at the news of Graham's death. What a slime-bucket. He sat glued to her side, asking if she wanted more wine, more bread, more hollandaise for her broccoli. For a minute, I thought he was going to lean over and cut her meat for her.

Robbie, barely concealing his disgust, watched as Kyle slobbered over her.

I looked for traces of the torrid affair I'd witnessed that afternoon between Kyle and Ms. Nesbitt, but those two were cool customers. There were no covert glances, no veiled smiles, no indication whatsoever that just hours ago they'd been frolicking in the bedsheets. The only time they talked to each other was when Nesbitt asked Kyle to please pass the butter.

I, meanwhile, was digging into my pork chops Florentine with gusto. One works up quite an appetite safecracking and sand-heisting. I was just about to plunge into the second chop when the conversation took an alarming turn.

"The most upsetting thing happened just before dinner," Nesbitt said. "When I went to my safe to get my pearls, it was open."

My fork froze en route to my mouth.

"Ours, too!" Maggie cried. "But nothing was stolen, thank heavens."

"I'm going to report it to the authorities," Nesbitt said.

"Oh, no need for that!" I piped up. "It happened to me, too. And I already reported it. Apparently a lot of the safes have been malfunctioning. They promised the problem would be fixed by the time dinner is over."

"That's a relief," Maggie sighed.

"Honestly!" Nesbitt sniffed. "For what they're charging on this cruise there should be no malfunctions."

"All's well that ends well—that's what I always say!" I chirped, determined to nip this let's-report-it-to-the-authorities thing in the bud.

"Jaine's right," Emily said, one of the few times she'd opened her mouth all night. "No need to make a fuss, Leona."

Thank heavens, I thought, returning to my pork chops. Crisis averted.

This one, anyway. There were plenty more about to hit my fan. But let's save those for another chapter, shall we?

Chapter 17

"Attention, muchachas and muchachos!" Paige's voice came over the PA as we filed out of the dining room. "You are all cordially invited to a gala Fiesta Party on the pool deck in fifteen minutes. Be there, or be square, amigos!"

"A fiesta!" Maggie exclaimed. "That sounds like fun!"

Two days ago, Emily would've been the first to agree with her, but now she stifled a yawn and said, "I think I'll be turning in."

"So soon?" Kyle asked with oily solicitousness. "Are you sure you don't want to go to the party?"

"I'm sure, dear. I just want to go to bed." Out of the flattering light of the dining room, her face was etched with wrinkles.

She bid everyone good night and walked away, clutching Leona's arm for support, unsure of her footing. This from a woman who just two nights ago was spinning around the dance floor. No doubt about it. Graham's death had aged her dramatically.

"Thank God," Kyle said, the minute they were gone. "The last thing I want is to hang out with a bunch of lowlifes at the fiesta party.

"C'mon, Maggie," he barked, back in drill sergeant mode. "We're going to the casino."

"Okay, honey." A forced smile from Maggie. "That should be fun. I haven't been gambling in ages."

Oh, boy. It looked like somebody was keeping her gambling addiction a secret from her husband.

"I guess that leaves just the two of us," Robbie said when they'd gone.

Which was fine with me. He looked awfully appealing in chinos and a baby blue oxford shirt.

"Do you feel like going to the fiesta party?" he asked.

I sensed a hesitancy in his voice.

"I'm up for it," I said. "But I'm not so sure you are."

"I'm just worried about Aunt Emily."

"I know what you mean. She does seem pretty depressed."

"The ship's doctor had to prescribe sleeping pills for her. He's even got Ms. Nesbitt spending the night on her sofa to keep an eye on her.

"But Kyle's probably right," he sighed. "Eventually she's bound to get over it, don't you think?"

"Of course," I assured him with a lot more confidence than I felt.

"And maybe in the end it's not such a bad thing," he said. "Maybe she'll look back and be grateful for those few extra days of happiness in her life." He seemed to brighten at the thought. "Anyhow, I guess it's a shame to let a good party go to waste. So what do you say? Are you ready to fiesta?"

"Sí, senor!"

Amazing, isn't it? Before dinner all I wanted was to dive into bed and sleep for the next twenty-four hours. And now, after one smile from Robbie, I was ready to fiesta the night away.

It was a crazy scene on the pool deck. The lounge chairs had been cleared away to make room for dancing, and gray-haired AARPsters were shaking their booties to rock and roll music spun by a deejay in a spandex tank top and giant sombrero. A smattering of young couples and teenagers were out there, too, gyrating their hips with the kind of wild abandon that comes only with well-lubricated joints.

Paige's social staff circled the crowd, handing out, of all things, Hawaiian leis. Don't ask me why they were handing out leis at a Mexican fiesta. Write Holiday Cruise Lines; maybe they can explain.

"Let's dance," Robbie said, taking me by the hand.

Uh-oh. Up to now we'd danced to old-fashioned slow tunes. Fast dances were a whole other story. I wasn't exactly up on the club scene (unless you count Sam's Club), and I didn't want to make a fool of myself.

But I looked around and figured, what the heck? Surely I couldn't be worse than the woman I saw doing the twist to what was clearly a cha-cha.

So I got out there and joined in the bootie-shaking.

At first I was a tad self-conscious, wishing I'd worn some flab-control panty hose, but the music was infectious, and after a while I stopped worrying about flying flab and started having fun.

Like me, Robbie was no expert on the dance floor, but what he lacked in skill he made up for in enthusiasm.

We'd just finished gyrating to a particularly frantic tune when Paige came up to the mike in a grass skirt and halter top, a cardigan thrown over her shoulders. I blinked at the sight of a grass skirt at a Mexican fiesta. Had no one on the social staff ever studied geography?

"Buenos notches, everybody," she called out in mangled Spanish. "Gather round, because it's time to play a fabulous game called Musical Men!"

Musical Men turned out to be a variation of Musical Chairs. Only instead of chairs, a bunch of men were lined up in a row. With music playing in the background, women contestants circled around them. When the music stopped, each woman had to find a man to hug. Whoever wound up without a man in her arms was eliminated. After every round, one of the jolly social staff got rid of one of the men, and another round began.

"Want to play?" Robbie asked after the rules were explained.

"Sure," I replied, eager to snatch a hug from him.

About ten men, most of them on the far side of Medicare, had volunteered to play the game and were now lined up like patients at a prostate testing center. A gaggle of women surrounded them.

We headed over to join them, and as we did I noticed Rita, my uber-irritating student and dedicated heckler. There she stood, next to her gal pals, her wiry hair glinting like Brillo.

We locked eyeballs, and I smiled a weak hello. But she did not return the smile. Instead, she turned to her buddies and began whispering what I was certain were unflattering comments about yours truly.

Oh, how I wanted to ace her out of this contest, I thought, as the music started up and the ladies began circling their prey.

I assessed my competition and figured it would be a piece of cake to latch on to a guy. After all, I was decades younger than most of these gals.

Wrong. Wrong. Wrong.

When the music stopped for the first time, it was like the running of the bulls in Pamplona. The stampede to the men was deafening. Luckily I managed to grab hold of a sweaty bald guy with a mind-blowing case of garlic breath.

"Hi, doll," he said, practically singeing my eyebrows.

Robbie stood just two men down from me, in the grip of a blue-haired senior. So close and yet so far.

The music started up again and once more lurched to a stop. And the stampede began. Most of these guys hadn't seen this much action in decades. This time I latched on to an elegant silver-haired gent whose hands wandered dangerously close to my tush.

I groaned when I glanced down the line and saw Rita clutching Robbie in a death grip. She turned to me and smirked.

I vowed to take her down before the night was through.

Using all the skills I'd learned outrunning kamikaze shoppers at Macy's 15-hour sale, I managed to stay in the game until there were just three women left: me, a disgustingly spry teenager, and—alas—Rita.

We were vying for the two remaining men: Robbie and the guy with the garlic breath.

The music started and we three gals began circling, eyeing each other warily. With only two guys left, surely I could make a run for Robbie. But when the music stopped, I was closest to Garlic Breath, so I hurled myself at him. Next to me, the teenager made a run for Robbie. She was just about to make contact when Rita burrowed in from the side and elbowed her out of the way in a move straight out of *Friday Night Smackdown.*

Rita clutched Robbie in victory as the teenager stalked off, muttering under her breath.

Now it was down to two men: Robbie and Garlic Breath.

The passengers voted on which of them was going to stay. Not surprisingly, Robbie won. Garlic Breath puffed off to the sidelines, leaving a miasma of halitosis in his wake.

Which left just me and Rita, fighting for Robbie.

The music began. I was determined to win. But how? Rita played dirty. I saw how she elbowed that poor teenager. If I wasn't careful, I could lose a kidney.

She was glaring at me now, circling Robbie like a caged tiger, her squinty eyes shooting death rays, her elbows poised to attack.

And then I got a brilliant idea. A stroke of genius, if I do say so myself.

Just as the music stopped, I pointed off to the side, shouting, "Look! It's Mary Higgins Clark!"

And in the brief instant it took Rita to turn and look, I flung myself onto Robbie, throwing my arms around his neck.

Victory! I had defeated the Most Irritating Woman in the World!

My victory was short-lived, however. Because

just then Paige stomped over in her grass skirt and cardigan, a frown marring her bland features.

"Ms. Austen," she snapped, "contests are for *paying* passengers only."

"Here you go," she said to Rita, handing her first prize, a fifty-dollar gift certificate to one of the ship's boutiques.

Rita just about broke the needle on the smirk-o-meter.

"Doesn't Jaine get anything?" Robbie piped up. "After all, she really was the winner."

Paige faked a smile for the paying customer. "Of course, sir."

"Here you go, Jaine," she said, handing me a cheesy ballpoint pen shaped like a maraca.

"Thanks," I said, shoving it in my pocket. "I'll treasure it forever."

"Well, I'm glad you're happy," she said, failing to detect the irony in my voice.

Then she headed back to the mike to continue emceeing the festivities.

As she walked away, something about her cardigan caught my eye. It was a bright chartreuse. I felt certain I'd seen it somewhere before.

And then I remembered. The second night of the cruise, when I'd come back from my brownie run, I'd seen a blonde in a nightgown and that same chartreuse cardigan slipping into Graham's cabin with a bottle of champagne. At the time I thought it was Cookie. But I was wrong. It was Paige.

So Cookie wasn't the only one having an affair with Graham. Paige had also been boffing the guy. Which means Paige was also jilted by him. What's more, Paige was there the day of Anton's ice sculpture demo. So she had access to his tools. Was it possible she flipped out when she learned of Graham's betrayal and sought revenge with Anton's ice pick?

"Jaine, are you okay?" Robbie asked as I stood there lost in thought.

"I'm fine," I said, adding another suspect to my ever-growing list.

Chapter 18

All thoughts of murder suspects quickly faded as the dancing started up again and once more I found myself making body contact with Robbie. The next few hours sailed by in a happy blur.

When the deejay had spun his last record, Robbie asked if I felt like getting a nightcap at the Tiki Lounge.

"Absolutely," I said, not wanting the evening to end.

We nabbed ourselves a cozy booth under a thatched umbrella and settled down with two margaritas and a bowl of mixed nuts. I studiously avoided the nuts, hoping to pass myself off as the kind of person who can sit across from a bowl of Planters' finest without inhaling it on contact.

"Here's to the real winner of the Musical Men contest," Robbie said, raising his glass in a toast.

"And to the last Musical Man standing," I added, fighting the impulse to scoot closer to his thighs.

There was no denying it. I was major league attracted to this guy.

I'd always pegged surfer types as beer-swilling dodos with marshmallows for brains. But Robbie was different. I wanted to learn more about him, hoping he'd live up to my hormones' expectations.

"So tell me how you got started making surfboards," I asked, grabbing a handful of the nuts I had not two seconds ago vowed not to touch.

"I've always loved the beach," he said, his eyes lighting up, "ever since I was a kid. I used to ride the bus two and a half hours to get to Santa Monica every weekend. So it's only natural I got into making surfboards. I can't think of anything I'd like doing better. It's my way of being creative."

Every day Robbie seemed less and less like the bad boy of my first impressions and more like the sensitive artist of my dreams. I suddenly had visions of the two of us in a cottage by the sea, Robbie carving his surfboards while I dashed off a Great American Novel or two.

"Yes, I'm a water baby, all right," he said. "Which reminds me—are you all set for scuba diving tomorrow?"

And just like that, my fantasy bubble popped.

I'd forgotten all about the darn scuba excursion. No way was I going to let my surfer prince see me in a bathing suit. But what excuse could I use to get out of it? Could I fake a sprained knee? Nah. Then I'd have to spend the rest of the cruise limping. Okay, how about a stomach flu? That wouldn't work either. Then I'd have to stop eating the nuts. Wait. I'd tell him I had an ear infection. That could work. People with ear infections weren't supposed to swim.

"Actually, Robbie—"

"Yes?"

Oh, hell. He looked so darn eager, I couldn't fink out on him. Heaven knows what strings he had to pull to get me on the excursion at the last minute. Or how much it cost. Some of those fancy excursions were nosebleed expensive.

"Actually," I said, caving yet again, "I can't wait either."

"That's great," he grinned.

Then he helped himself to a handful of nuts in the absentminded way naturally skinny people do.

"So now that you know I'm a surfaholic, what about you? What's your passion in life?"

I adroitly refrained from mentioning the first three answers that sprang to mind: milk chocolate, dark chocolate, and pepperoni pizza.

Instead, I said, "Oh, writing. Definitely."

"I've always been in awe of writers."

I smiled modestly, hoping he wouldn't remember that I spent most of my days writing about toilet bowls.

We hung around the bar for a while longer, sharing tidbits from our lives (mine carefully edited). When we'd licked the last of the salt from the rims of our margarita glasses, Robbie said, "Well, I guess it's time to call it a night."

"I guess so."

He hesitated a beat.

"Say, why don't I walk you back to your cabin?"

Whoa. You know what that meant, don't you? It was the nautical equivalent of *Your place or mine?* Well, if he thought I was going to leap in the sack with him he had another thing coming. I wasn't about to get frisky with him this early in the game. Not with my principles, not with my ethics—and not with my cat stowed illegally in my cabin.

But maybe I was jumping to conclusions. Maybe he had nothing more licentious on his mind than a good-night kiss.

Which sounded awfully appealing to me. It couldn't hurt to try for a good-night kiss, could it?

Up to now Robbie and I had been chattering like jaybirds, but as we headed down the corridor to my cabin, we fell silent.

I was desperately trying to think of something clever to say, but not a single conversational gambit cropped up in my allegedly creative brain.

"Here we are," I squeaked, when we finally reached my cabin.

I looked up and saw that Robbie was staring at me. For once his lopsided grin was nowhere to be found. Indeed he looked quite serious when he said, "You know, Jaine, I really like you."

"I do, too! Like you, that is, not me. Not that I don't like myself. Of course I do, although sometimes I can be rough on myself, self-critical, you know. I've really got to work on that—"

Oh, for crying out loud. Of all times to start babbling.

"I know what you meant, Jaine," he said, touching his finger to my lips.

This was it. The moment I'd been waiting for since I first saw him buttering a French roll in the dining room. He was leaning in to kiss me!

Then, just as our lips were about to meet, I looked over his shoulder and saw something that made my blood freeze.

It was Prozac, peeking out from behind an alcove!

Dammit! She must've sneaked out when Samoa came in to turn down the bed. I should've known it was only a matter of time before she made a break for it.

"Oh, no!" I cried, pulling away.

"What's wrong?" Robbie asked.

Time for some fast talking.

"Um, I lost my earrings!" I clutched my earlobes as if I'd just realized the earrings were missing.

"Let's go look for them," I said, yanking him down the corridor as fast and as far away from Prozac as possible.

"I didn't realize you were wearing earrings," he said, as we raced along.

"They're very small. You probably didn't notice them. They must've fallen off while we were dancing. They mean so much to me; my grandmother gave them to me on her deathbed. In fact, her dying words were, *'Jaine, whatever you do, don't lose the earrings . . .'* "

Clearly the lobe in my brain in charge of idiotic babbling was in overdrive.

"I totally understand," Robbie said, as we reached the elevators.

I jabbed the elevator button, terrified I was going to see Prozac prancing into view.

It seemed like centuries before the dratted contraption finally showed up. I leapt on eagerly, and then, just as the doors were about to shut, I pressed the DOOR OPEN button and scooted out again.

"Guess what?" I cried. "I found my earrings. They were in my pocket all along."

"They were?" Robbie said, quite justifiably looking at me as if I had more than a few screws loose.

"Well, nighty night!" I chirped.

And as the elevators closed on Robbie's stupefied face, I raced off in search of my escaped stowaway.

I found the little devil at the end of the corridor, chowing down on the remains of someone's room service dinner.

"What do you think you're doing?" I hissed, snatching her up in my arms.

She shot me an affronted glare.

Hey, wait! I haven't finished those fries.

I hustled her back to my cabin and was just about to put the key in the slot when I heard, "Well, hellooo, kitty."

Oh, groan. I'd recognize that smarmy voice anywhere.

I turned to see Anton, decked out in an eye-popping outfit of orange Bermuda shorts, Day-Glo Hawaiian shirt, and—his pièce de résistance—black socks with sandals.

"Last I heard," he said, eyeing Prozac, "cats weren't allowed on board."

"Gorillas aren't either, but they let you on."

Okay, so I wasn't dumb enough to say that.

"How on earth did you find my cabin?" were the words that actually came out of my mouth.

"I've been following you all night."

Not *all* night. Clearly he'd taken some time off to rendezvous with his buddy Jack Daniels. The guy reeked of booze.

"Aren't you afraid someone's going to report your kitty to the authorities?" he asked, scratching Prozac behind her ears.

The little slut purred in ecstasy.

"Aw, c'mon, Anton." With Herculean effort, I managed a smile. "You're not going to tell anyone, are you?"

"That depends," he leered, "on whether you invite me in for a little mattress action."

Yuck. I'd rather suck a slug.

But just then I saw another couple coming down the hallway. Panicked lest they see Prozac, I opened the cabin and dragged Anton inside.

"I knew all along you were into me, babe," he preened. "Just playing hard to get, huh?"

"Forget it, Anton," I said, tossing Prozac onto the bed and barricading myself behind the cabin's only chair. "No way on earth am I going to sleep with you."

"How about some heavy petting?"

"Ain't gonna happen."

"Okay, then. I'm going to tell. One word from me and the cat's in quarantine."

He started for the door.

I should have let him go. I'd jumped through enough hoops for my spoiled feline princess, who was now sprawled out on the bed licking her privates, no doubt dreaming about her next snack. But you know what a softie I am when it comes to Prozac. I couldn't let Anton turn her in.

"Wait a minute!" I called out, wracking my brain for a way to keep him quiet. "I don't suppose you have a book you'd like me to edit?"

He shook his head.

"A screenplay? Surely you have an idea for a screenplay. Nine out of ten men with ponytails do."

"Sorry, babe. The only idea I have involves you and me between the sheets. So whaddaya say?"

And then, as a preview of coming attractions, he whipped off his Hawaiian shirt.

I gasped. Not at the sight of his hairy belly. Or his rusty nipple studs. (Although Lord knows they were gaspworthy.)

No, what had me transfixed was a large technicolor tattoo on his chest. And not just any tattoo. But a tattoo of a butterfly.

A gold star to those of you who guessed what that meant.

"Omigosh," I blurted out. "You're the Butterfly Bandit!"

And just like that, he sobered up.

"How did you find out?" he asked warily.

"I saw the newspaper clipping in Graham's wallet."

"That was a long time ago, Jaine. I've cleaned up my act since then."

"Graham was blackmailing you, wasn't he?"

"Yeah, he was blackmailing me," he said through gritted teeth. "Threatened to tell the cruise line about my checkered past."

A shiver of fear ran down my spine. Had Anton killed Graham to shut him up? Was I alone in my cabin with a half-naked, hairy-bellied killer?

"But I didn't kill him, if that's what you're thinking."

He shot me one of his meant-to-be-sexy smiles, but this time there was something forced about it.

"C'mon, doll. You don't really think I'm the kind of guy who'd kill someone?"

Of course I did! Why hadn't I thought of it before? What if no one had stolen Anton's ice picks? What if he'd just pretended they were missing to throw suspicion off himself? I thought of how he'd complained to me that day on the deck, telling me the ice picks were gone from his case. But maybe he just wanted everyone to *think* they were stolen—so that when Graham showed up with one of them plunged in his chest, no one would suspect the seemingly foolish ice sculptor.

He didn't seem the least bit foolish now, I thought, eyeing his thick chest and brawny arms.

"You believe me, don't you?" he asked, with a feral smile.

"Sure," I lied.

"And you're not going to tell anyone?"

"I'll make you a deal," I said, trying not to show my growing fear. "If you don't tell about my cat, I won't tell about the Butterfly Bandit."

"Okay," he said. "Deal. Sure you don't want to seal it with a kiss?"

"I don't think so."

I could tell he didn't really want to either. No, by now he was playing a part. His eyes were no longer hazy with desire, but focused and calculating.

I'd finally succeeded in dampening his libido.

And as he picked up his shirt and headed out into the corridor, I suddenly remembered that there had been two ice picks "stolen" from his supplies. You know what that means, don't you?

One of them was still out there, ready and available for getting rid of pesky P.I.s.

YOU'VE GOT MAIL

To: Jaineausten
From: DaddyO
Subject: Good as New

I just finished staining the floor, lambchop, and if I do say so myself, I did a magnificent job! You'd never guess in a million years there'd ever been any paint there. Even your mother had to admit it looks pretty darn terrific.

Love and kisses,

Your daddy,

"Handy" Hank Austen

To: Jaineausten
From: Shoptillyoudrop
Subject: A Minor Miracle

You won't believe this, honey, but Daddy actually managed to stain the floor without spilling anything! Talk about your minor miracles! Now he's strutting around the apartment, puffing on that dratted pipe of his, talking about his "inner craftsman." Heavens. The way he's carrying on, you'd think he'd just painted the Sistine Chapel.

Meanwhile, Lance and I are headed off to check out wedding cakes. I asked Daddy to come with us, but he wants to stay home like an old fuddy-dud and watch golf on TV.

Do you realize how lucky you are to have found a man who actually enjoys the fun things in life like wedding planning? Oh, I just know you two are going to be so happy together!

XXX,

Mom

PS. I ordered you a fabulous peignoir from the shopping channel. Perfect for your honeymoon. It has adorable pink sequined hearts all over the bodice. The show host said the Duchess of Windsor wore one just like it on her honeymoon!

To: Jaineausten
From: DaddyO
Subject: Home Improvement

Your mom and Lance just left to check out wedding cakes. Those two sure are hitting it off. You'd better watch out she doesn't steal him away from you. Ha-ha.

By the way, lambchop, I've been taking a good

look around your apartment and I see a lot of home improvement projects I could tackle while I'm here. Track lighting, for one. Marvin, the guy down at the hardware store, says it's all the rage. And how about some new plumbing fixtures in your bathroom? Those should be a snap to install.

Yep, as long as I'm here I may as well put my Inner Craftsman to good use and spruce your place up. It's the least I can do for my little lamb-chop!

XXX,

Daddy

**To: Jaineausten
From: Shoptillyoudrop
Subject: Chocolate or Strawberry?**

Lance and I just got back from looking at the most gorgeous wedding cakes! Honestly, I've never seen anything like them. My favorite was a devil's food castle—surrounded by a moat of hot fudge! Doesn't that sound yummy?

The baker was such a charming man. And very attractive. He and Lance hit it off so well, I wouldn't be surprised if he gave us a discount, too! It's just wonderful how Lance has won everyone over!

Now you have to decide about the cake. Which do you like better? Devil's food with chocolate crème filling? Or lemon with strawberry? Oh, why am I even asking? I already know the answer. Chocolate it is!

Love from your very excited,

Mom

To: Jaineausten
From: DaddyO

Just ran out to the hardware store and picked up the plumbing fixtures. Wait'll you see them, lambchop! The faucets are shaped like beer kegs! Nifty, huh? Marvin said it's what all the trendy decorators are using. And did I tell you he's giving me a Frequent Buyer Discount?

I'll get started first thing in the morning. In the meanwhile, time to sit back and relax with my pipe.

Love & kisses,

Daddy

To: Jaineausten
From: Sir Lancelot
Subject: Wild Idea

Jaine, sweetie, I had no idea the wedding industry was so packed full of eligibles. You should've seen the baker we met today. To die for! I swear, getting engaged to you has been the best thing to happen to my love life since spandex bike shorts.

Don't kill me, but I didn't tell your mom the truth.

In fact, she and I are having so much fun planning this wedding, I've just had a wild idea: Why don't we go through with it? I mean, I've always dreamed of a beachside wedding. We won't stay married, of course. Once we split up, I can start dating all the men I've met. And we'll cash in the wedding gifts and reimburse your parents for what they spent. This way your mom and I get to have the wedding of our dreams, and you get to have a devil's food wedding cake with a hot fudge moat. What do you say? Does it work for you?

XXX,

Lance

Chapter 19

I swear, Marian, I saw a cat!"

I was standing in the elevator the next morning when I heard those alarming words. I turned to see a middle-aged couple in Holiday Cruise Lines sweatshirts.

The man, a florid guy with a drinker's web of broken capillaries on his nose, was clearly agitated.

"A cat!" he repeated, in case his wife didn't get it the first time.

"Don't be silly, Fred," she replied, checking her hair in the elevator's mirrored walls.

"I'm telling you, Marian, I saw that cat as clear as day. It was right outside our door eating french fries."

Oh, crud. The last thing I needed was this guy broadcasting news of Prozac's midnight escapades. Thank heavens there was no one else in the elevator. But what if his wife believed him? What if they went racing off to the authorities and they did a cabin-to-cabin search looking for Prozac?

"It was probably just a shadow," his wife said, now wiping a lipstick smudge from her teeth. "That's what you get for drinking so many martinis last night."

"But it looked so real." Suddenly he sounded a lot less sure of himself.

"Remember the time you thought you saw a mountain lion in our garage and it turned out to be your exercycle?"

He nodded, abashed.

"Tonight you're having one glass of wine with dinner. And that's it."

"Yes, Marian."

I breathed a sigh of relief. Thank heavens for henpecked husbands.

The moment of truth had arrived. I could put it off no longer. Like it or not, I had to buy a bathing suit for that dratted scuba excursion.

(*WARNING: Sensitive readers beware. Graphic tush-in-three-way-mirror scene ahead.*)

I made my way to the ship's clothing boutique, where I was greeted by a tiny redheaded sprite. I'm guessing she was about a size zero soaking wet. I hadn't even tried anything on, and I was depressed already.

There ought to be a law about bathing suit sales-people. Only nice motherly women with generous hips should be allowed to sell them. Not tiny slip-of-a-thing sprites.

"How may I help you today?" She smiled perkily. I'd be perky, too, if I had a torso the size of a Pringles can.

"I need a bathing suit."

Minutes later I was trapped in front of a three-way mirror (don't say I didn't warn you) in a dowdy black number that looked like it was designed by the same mortician who'd come up with my outfit for formal night.

It was a choice between that and a hot pink tankini that left nothing to the imagination except thoughts of suicide.

"See how it takes inches off your waist?" the sprite gushed as I stared at my image in dismay.

Yes, indeedie, it did. Unfortunately, it shoved those inches right down to my hips, which had all the inches they needed, thank you very much.

"Are these all you've got?" I asked.

"I'll go check and see what else is out there."

Soon she was back in the dressing room holding up a red floral monstrosity.

"How about this one? It's got a special compartment for incontinence pads."

"I guess I'll stick with the one I'm wearing."

"I think you'll like it. We sell a lot of them to nuns."

And ninety dollars later I was walking out of the shop with my black nunsuit.

I was a lot less depressed than I would normally be under the circumstances. Mainly because I was too busy worrying about that missing ice pick. Needless to say, I'd had a hard time falling asleep after Anton's visit to my cabin last night. I'd just laid there, my head resting on the tiny bit of pillow that Prozac had grudgingly allotted me, wondering if Anton could possibly be the murderer-at-large on the SS *Festival*.

Of course, he was just one of my many viable suspects. If only I could figure out which of them was the killer.

After a while I turned on the light and did what I often do when faced with a thorny problem. I grabbed a pen and paper and began writing. Writing, I find, like fine chocolate, often helps clarify my thoughts.

For the record, here's what I wrote:

My Suspects
By Jaine Austen

Anton. *AKA the Butterfly Bandit. The latest entry in my suspect sweepstakes. Graham's blackmail victim. And a man with a known criminal history. In addition to bank robbery and numerous fashion crimes, had he used his own ice pick to stab his blackmailer to death?*

Kyle Pritchard. *The Suspect I'd Most Like to See Behind Bars. Desperate to keep his hands on Emily's money. Threatened to do whatever it took to keep Graham from marrying Emily. Did that include murder? (True, I didn't find the cuff links in his safe. But maybe I was wrong about the cuff links. Maybe the killer didn't take them, after all. Or maybe I was just a lousy cabin searcher.)*

Leona Nesbitt. *Another juicy suspect.*

Graham had threatened to fire her. Did she kill him to save her job? Was she in cahoots—both in and out of bed—with Kyle? And what about those damp shoes? Did she get them out on deck plunging an ice pick into Graham's heart?

__Maggie Pritchard.__ Mousy on the outside, but a killer on the inside? Compulsive gambler with a nasty habit to feed. Had she wiped out Graham to protect her source of chips?

__Chips.__ Wonder if they have any down at the buffet. Yes, chips would be nice right now—with some melted cheese—and maybe some guacamole—

Okay, so my mind wandered a tad. But you'll be happy to know I did not go tearing down to the buffet for nachos. I couldn't possibly allow one more empty calorie past my lips, not when I had to show up in front of Robbie in a bathing suit. So for once I reined in the tapeworm that resides in my stomach and went back to bed.

After a while, with the sweet sounds of Prozac snoring in my ear, I finally drifted off into an uneasy sleep.

Sad to say, when I woke up this morning, I was just as confused as ever. Writing down my thoughts had brought me no clarity whatsoever. All I knew for sure was that my murderer-at-large was still very much at large.

With that happy thought bouncing around my brain, I set off for a fun day of scuba diving.

I'd arranged to meet the Pritchards for lunch in Cabo before heading off for our scuba adventure. Heaven knows where those sports nuts had been all morning. Probably squeezing in a triathlon.

Unfortunately, I had to take a cab to the restaurant where we were meeting. I found the cheapest taxi available, a rattletrap VW Beetle that had been around since Goebbels was in diapers, and forked over twenty-two bucks for the privilege of bumping along in a miasma of exhaust fumes.

At last we arrived at our destination, a charming hacienda-style restaurant awash in hot pink bougainvillea, with a spectacular view of Cabo San Lucas Bay. As I walked up the steps to the front patio I could hear the sounds of strolling mariachis inside.

I checked at the front desk, but the Pritchards had not yet arrived.

So I went back outside and called Lance on my cell. I dreaded to think what a long-distance international phone call would cost, but I'd checked my e-mails that morning and was determined to call a halt to our impending "wedding" before the invitations went out.

Thank heavens he picked up.

"Hi, sweetie," he said, his voice faint but bubbly with excitement. "Your mom and I just got back from interviewing the most amazing florist. What a hottie! Fabulous abs, and peonies to die for! That's what we're going with for the wedding, by the way. Peonies."

"Lance!" I shouted into the phone. Our connection wasn't all that great and I had to cover my exposed ear to block out the sound from the mariachis. "There will be no peonies! There will be no wedding! I insist that you tell my mother the truth!"

"But, Jaine," he whined, "I'm meeting so many great guys."

"I don't care how many guys you're meeting, you've got to tell my mother the wedding is off."

"Are you sure you don't want to go through with it? I'll invite some straight guys. You might meet somebody, too!"

"Forget it, Lance. I do not intend to go trolling for dates at my own wedding."

"Oh, all right," he sulked.

"Promise you'll tell my mom the truth?"

"I promise, I promise." Then grudgingly he asked, "So how's the cruise? Having fun?"

"Not exactly."

"I told you it would be a disaster!" he gloated. "I want all the details."

And before I knew it, I was spilling my guts to him at about a zillion dollars a minute, telling him all about Graham's murder.

"It's been incredibly frustrating. The captain

won't listen to a thing I say. The minute we get back to L.A. I'm going to the police and tell them everything I know."

"Just be careful, okay?"

"Oh, I will. But I'd better hang up now, before I need a cosigner to pay my phone bill. And tell Daddy I absolutely forbid him to do one more repair on my apartment!"

"Will do. Oops. Gotta go. There's your mom on the other line."

I hung up, and the minute I did, I realized I had company. I turned to see the Pritchards standing just a few feet away from me. I hadn't heard them coming over the noise of the mariachis.

Damn. What if they heard me yapping about the murder? I scanned their faces, checking their reactions. Kyle and Nesbitt were glaring at me, but then they were always glaring at me. Robbie was smiling tentatively. (At least he was smiling—which was more than I deserved after my nutty behavior last night.) And Maggie wasn't looking at me at all, busy applying sunblock to her already red nose.

I was happy to see that Emily had made it out of her cabin and had joined them on their expedition. She stood at Nesbitt's side, staring vacantly out to sea.

"Gee, I didn't know you guys were here."

"We were waiting for you to finish your phone call," Nesbitt snapped.

Emily turned to me with a wan smile.

"Don't worry, dear," she said. "We haven't been waiting long."

As we headed into the dining room Robbie pulled me aside.

"Are you okay?" he whispered.

"Sure."

"I only ask because you were acting sort of strange last night."

Strange? Moi? Just because I was hopping on and off an elevator like a bipolar bunny?

"Oh, no, I'm fine. Just fine."

I plastered on my brightest smile.

"Good," he said, gracing me with a high-octane grin of his own. "Glad to hear it. And I'm glad you found them."

"Found what?"

"Your earrings."

"Oh, right. My earrings. Of course."

My God, Jaine. Pay attention!

We joined the others at a primo window table with a breathtaking view of the water below.

A bevy of waiters and busboys descended on us, passing out menus, wine lists, rolls, and bottled water.

I opened the menu and, like a high-cholesterol homing pigeon, zeroed in on the Petit Filet Mignon. For days I'd been lusting after a nice juicy steak. And there it was—just the way I liked it—with shoestring fries and crisp onion rings.

But I couldn't possibly order it. It was the most expensive thing on the menu. And I'd be nuts to eat a big meal before putting on a bathing suit. My waist could not afford to expand one more millimeter. No, I'd do the sensible thing and get a healthy green salad, hold the dressing.

"And for you, senorita?"

The waiter was at my side, his pad at the ready.

"I'll have the filet mignon."

I know. I'm impossible. But what the heck? Once Robbie saw me in my nunsuit, it was all over anyway. What did it matter if I had a steak and fries under my belt?

"Are you crazy?" Kyle squawked. "A steak before scuba diving? You want to sink like an anchor?"

"Most unwise," Nesbitt chimed in, lips pursed in disapproval.

"Actually," Robbie said, shooting me an apologetic smile, "it's probably not the best idea."

With heavy heart, I kissed my steak good-bye and ordered the Cabo salad, which turned out to be an anemic plate of greens and veggies with a few shards of shredded chicken on top.

"So how did you spend your morning, Jaine?" Maggie asked as I rooted around my salad in search of croutons.

"Oh, just lazing around," I said, saving the details of my bathing suit fiasco for a therapist. "What were you guys up to?"

"We went on a tour of a factory where we watched the artists make handblown glass. So fascinating!"

"Yes, that was interesting, wasn't it?" Emily said, a spark of her old enthusiasm returning to her voice. "I've always loved glass collectibles. Remember that wonderful factory outside of Venice, Leona? Such beautiful goblets. Graham and I are going to stop off there on our honeymoo—"

She blinked in confusion.

"Oh, dear. For a moment I forgot."

Then tears sprang to her eyes as she remembered that she and Graham were going nowhere together.

"Excuse me, everyone," she said, her voice cracking. "I need to powder my nose."

"I'll go with you," Nesbitt said.

"No, you stay here, dear. I'd rather be alone."

And with that, she got up from the table and hurried toward the ladies' room.

"Poor thing," Maggie sighed.

"Time heals all wounds," Nesbitt intoned solemnly, as if she'd come up with that ditty on her own.

"Ms. Nesbitt is right," Kyle said. "By next week, she'll have forgotten all about it."

Robbie shook his head, disgusted. "You're an idiot, Kyle."

Hear, hear! I felt like shouting.

"I won't dignify that with a response," Kyle said.

The two brothers exchanged glares as the mariachis played gaily in the background. Everyone proceeded to pick at their food—everyone except Kyle, who wasn't going to let his aunt's tears get in the way of his lunch. I gave up my search for croutons in my salad and wasn't at all sad to bid it adieu when one of the busboys whisked it away.

After a while Emily returned to the table, her eyes red-rimmed from crying.

Kyle put on his caring face.

"Are you okay, Aunt Em?"

"I'm fine." She forced a smile.

"You know what they say," he cooed, taking her hand in his. "Everything always happens for the best. I wasn't going to tell you, but I had Graham checked out by a detective agency. They e-mailed me their report this morning. He was a complete fraud." This said with a smug nod. "Never worked at British Petroleum. Was a ship's steward all his life. Cleaned toilets for a living.

"I hate to say this, Auntie," he went on, not hating it at all, "but all he wanted was your money."

Emily sat up rigid in her chair.

"Then you two had a lot in common," she said, yanking her hand from his.

Kyle blanched under his country club tan.

"You think I don't know what you're really

like?" Emily said, with glacial calm. "Fawning all over me, counting the days till I die and you inherit my money. I understand you all too well, Kyle. And now it's time you understood me."

By now Kyle's jaw was slack with disbelief.

"You say one more word against the man I loved, and you'll never see another penny of my money again. Is that clear?"

He nodded numbly.

Then Emily picked up her spoon and calmly began stirring her coffee.

Way to go, Aunt Em!

If I could, I would've given her a standing ovation.

Chapter 20

We rode over to our "Scuba Adventure" in a private van the Pritchards had hired for the day. I sat next to Robbie in the backseat, hoping he couldn't hear my stomach growling. It wasn't used to salad for lunch.

I nodded intently as he talked about a scuba expedition he'd taken in Tahiti, but I didn't hear a word, my mind paralyzed at the thought of my impending doom.

Any minute now he'd be getting his first look at me and my cellulite in my nunsuit. I could practically see cupid putting away his bow and arrow and heading off to greener pastures.

All too soon we got to the beach and were herded off to cabanas to change.

The good news is I did *not* have to appear in public in an unflattering bathing suit.

That's because my unflattering bathing suit was hidden underneath an even more unflattering wet suit, a black neoprene monstrosity that revealed every lump and bump in my body.

Why oh why hadn't I come up with an excuse to get out of this damn excursion?

I prayed for a shark sighting, an earthquake, a tsunami—anything to shut down the beach.

When Mother Nature did not oblige with any natural disasters, I took a deep breath and headed out to join the others.

It was a blazingly hot day and the beach was crowded with tourists and locals alike.

Instantly I began sweating in my neoprene straightjacket.

My only consolation, I thought, as I trudged along in the sand, was that at least the less-than-svelte Maggie would look as ghastly as I did.

But then I saw her, still in her street clothes, stretched out alongside Emily in a comfy lounge chair under the shade of a huge thatched umbrella. I wasn't surprised to see Emily sitting it out. But what was Maggie doing here?

"Aren't you going diving?" I asked her as I approached their umbrella.

"I decided to keep Aunt Emily company."

What a great excuse. Why hadn't I thought of it? How I longed to change back into my elastic-waist shorts and plop down next to them.

"Have a good dive, dear!" Emily said.

"Oh, I will," I lied with a sick smile.

Still praying for a last-minute tsunami, I trekked off to join the other Pritchards. They were standing at the shore with the rest of the tour divers—all of whom were in depressingly better shape than I was. One of the gals, a hawk-faced dame with abs of steel, smugly announced that it was her eightieth birthday. This is what she did on her eightieth birthday? Had the woman never heard of birthday cake and margaritas?

I studiously avoided eye contact with Robbie, afraid of the disappointment I was bound to see in his eyes. I couldn't help taking a peek at his bod, though, which was taut and trim. As was Ms. Nesbitt's. I was hoping she'd have at least a love handle or two. But she was sculpted tight as a drum, probably from all those hours of sexual calisthenics. Only Kyle showed signs of a burgeoning martini belly.

Miguel, our bronzed Adonis of a scuba instructor, looked me over and frowned.

"I take it you've never been scuba diving before."

"Oh, yes, scads of times. Why do you ask?"

"You've got your wet suit on backward."

Oh, groan. How could I have been such an idiot?

"Um. That's the way we wear them in Hermosa," I said, referring to my hometown of Hermosa Beach.

"I'm sorry, but you can't wear it that way here."

"I'll go back to my cabana and change."

"We really don't have time for that," Miguel said, checking his watch.

And so, in a moment that haunts my dreams to this day, I had to stand there in front of everyone and struggle out of my wet suit. Which meant that Robbie got to see me in my nunsuit, after all.

As I righted my wet suit faux pas, Miguel began handing out the rest of our scuba gear. I never realized there was so much involved in a simple dip underwater. It's all très technical, so I won't bore you with the details, but eventually I wound up with an air tank strapped to my back and enough connecting hoses to open my own garden supply store.

Around my waist I wore a tire-like contraption to keep me afloat. (Just what I needed—more inches!) Top it all off with fins and face mask, and voila—instant Creature from the Black Lagoon.

When we were all strapped in and hosed up, Miguel gathered us around in a circle.

"I realize you're all experienced divers," Miguel said, with a dubious glance in my direction, "but I want to go over a few basic rules before we begin."

I paid frantic attention to the basic rules. The most important of which was to press a little doohickey on my wrist (known as the "regulator" to bona fide scuba divers) when I needed air from the tank strapped to my back.

"All set, everybody?" Miguel said when he was through. "Are we ready for some fun?"

The only thing I was ready for was a nap. And possibly a brownie or three.

"You okay, Jaine?" Robbie asked as we waded out into the water.

"I'm fine," I assured him, still not making eye contact.

By now we'd reached the sandbar where the water suddenly got deeper.

"Let's do it!" Miguel shouted. "Follow me."

This was it. Zero hour. I said a quick prayer and took the plunge.

Thanks to swimming lessons as a child (where I first discovered that Mr. Bathing Suit was not my friend), I already knew how to dive underwater. So I was actually able to follow the others.

Much to my relief, I managed to work the regulator thingie on my wrist, sending air through a hose to my mouth as I needed it. It took a minute or two to get used to breathing through my mouthpiece, but soon I began to relax and enjoy myself. All sorts of amazing fish were swimming past me.

Then Robbie swam up to me and waved. I waved back.

Gee, this was fun. Maybe I had an aptitude for

water sports after all. Could I possibly have a future with Robbie? Who knew? Maybe he liked a gal with a few extra pounds under her wet suit.

Before long I was lost in a fantasy of me and Robbie frolicking at the beach, running hand in hand across the sand to our cottage by the sea, where, after frantic whoopsy doodle, we'd cuddle together sharing a pint of Chunky Monkey. (Okay, a quart of Chunky Monkey.)

I was in the midst of deciding what to name our first child—Owen, if it was a boy, Marissa or Heidi, if it was a girl—when I suddenly realized the others were nowhere in sight.

They must've dived down deeper. I briefly considered trying to find them, but no way was I going any deeper, not by myself. It was probably time I got out of the water anyway.

I was just about to head back up to the surface when I felt someone moving behind me. Before I could turn to see who it was, I felt a sharp tug on my air hose. And the next thing I knew, the hose was floating in front of my face mask—severed from my air tank.

Omigod! My air supply had been cut off! Suddenly water was rushing in through the remaining stub of hose in my mouth.

I spat out my mouthpiece and struggled to the surface holding my breath, my heart racing wildly. I didn't think I'd gone down far at all, but now it seemed to take forever to get back up. By the time my head finally emerged from the water, it felt like my lungs were going to burst.

Frantically I gasped for air, sucking it up in enormous gulps.

Then, with trembling limbs, I paddled to the sandbar and waded back to shore.

If I wasn't mistaken, the killer had just struck again.

Emily and Maggie hurried to my side as I staggered out of the water.

"Jaine, dear!" Emily cried. "What on earth happened?"

But all I could do was cough in reply.

Now the others began emerging from their dive. Soon they were all huddled in a circle around me.

"What's going on here?" Miguel wanted to know.

"Someone tried to kill me," I said, my voice hoarse from coughing.

"That can't be!" Emily's eyes were wide with disbelief.

"Someone swam up behind me and cut my air hose. Look."

I showed everyone the severed cord.

"Do you suppose a fish could have bitten it?" Maggie asked.

"Don't be absurd," Nesbitt snapped. "It was probably one of the locals."

She gazed in disdain at a Mexican family playing in the sand.

"Really, Leona," Emily said. "Why would a local want to harm Jaine?"

"They're hot-blooded Latins. You never know what they'll do."

Miguel shot her a livid look. In case she forgot, he was one of those "hot-blooded Latins."

"It looks to me like she may have cut it on a rock," he said, running his finger along the severed edge.

What a crock. He just didn't want an attempted murder on his watch.

"I was nowhere near a rock!"

"I think we should call the police," one of the others suggested.

"We don't have time to call the police," Nesbitt scoffed. "We have to be back on ship in less than an hour."

"You never should've allowed her on the tour," the eightieth-birthday girl scolded Miguel. "She clearly wasn't experienced. Anyone could tell she didn't know what she was doing."

I wished she'd stop talking about me like I wasn't there.

"It's my fault," Robbie said. "I should have been watching you, Jaine. I thought you were following us, and by the time I realized I'd lost you, it was too late. I'm so sorry."

For the first time since I put on my wet suit, I

looked into Robbie's eyes, and they seemed to be filled with genuine concern.

In the end, we did not call the police. Nesbitt was right. We simply didn't have time. Instead, we trudged back up to our cabanas to change out of our wet suits.

And as we walked along in the sand it suddenly occurred to me that there was someone missing from the circle of people who'd surrounded me.

"Where's Kyle?" I asked.

"He must've gone ahead to change," Maggie said.

Very interesting. Kyle Pritchard was the one person who didn't come over to find out what happened to me. Maybe because he was there when it happened.

To hell with Paige and her rules. No way was I joining the others for dinner that night. I was convinced Kyle was the one who tried to drown me that afternoon, and I was not about to break bread with the guy.

Instead, I stayed huddled in bed with Prozac, eating a roast beef panini I'd brought back from the buffet.

"Oh, Pro, it was so awful," I moaned, unable to forget my near brush with death.

She'd long since inhaled the whitefish I'd brought for her dinner and was now eyeing my sandwich hungrily.

"Suddenly all that water came rushing in through my air hose, and I couldn't breathe!"

Yeah, whatever. Can I have some of that roast beef?

She thrust her pink nose at it eagerly.

"Oh, for crying out loud. Just once, can't you show a little sympathy?"

I scooped out a hunk of meat and put it on her plate.

Gone in sixty seconds. So I gave her some more. I was lucky she let me eat the roll.

I polished off the few remaining crumbs from my plate and spent the next few hours staring glassily at a movie on TV. But I couldn't concentrate. For all I knew, it could've been a test pattern.

Finally, I turned out the light, but sleep didn't come. I couldn't shake the awful memory of that water rushing in through my air hose. Figuring a glass of wine might help me relax, I threw on my jeans and a sweatshirt and set out in search of liquid comfort.

I wandered into the first bar I came across, a dimly lit lounge with leather booths and soft music tinkling in the background. The place was fairly deserted. Everybody was probably off watching the entertainment in the Grand Showroom.

I took a seat at the bar and ordered a chardonnay from a sleepy-looking bartender.

Just as he was bringing it to me, I heard someone call my name.

"Yoo hoo, Jaine!"

I looked up and saw Maggie getting up from one of the leather booths. I checked the booth for signs of Kyle, but thank heavens he wasn't there.

Maggie lurched across the room unsteadily, drink in hand, and plopped down next to me at the bar.

If she was concerned about my recent brush with death, she showed no signs of it.

"You really should try one of these," she said, pointing to her elaborate umbrella drink.

From the way she was slurring her words—and from the two paper umbrellas stuck in her hair—I got the distinct impression this was not her first drink of the evening.

"A toast," she said, raising her concoction aloft. "To my upcoming divorce!"

"Your divorce?"

I blinked in surprise. Not that I blamed her for wanting out from her marriage. I just didn't think she'd have the nerve to cut lose.

"To my miserable rat of a husband," she continued, still in toastmaster mode. "May he fly tourist class straight to hell!"

Hello. There was a story here, and, her tongue well oiled by booze, Maggie was about to tell it.

"Would you believe Kyle's been cheating on me with that prune Leona Nesbitt?"

"No!" I said, doing my best to look shocked.

"I thought something was fishy when he ditched

the tour in Mazatlan. Said he had a headache. Trust me—Kyle doesn't get headaches. He gives them.

"So I ditched the tour, too, and followed him back to the ship. Just as I was getting off the elevator I saw him slipping into her cabin. I heard those two moaning and groaning all the way down the hallway. *Oh, Kylesie! You're the best!* The best?? Puh-leese! I've had sneezes that lasted longer than Kyle."

Oh, my. This was quite an earful, wasn't it?

"And then today," she said, tucking the paper umbrella from her drink alongside the others in her hair, "when I checked his e-mails in the ship's computer room, I found out the two of them are planning to run off together.

"To think," she sputtered, "that I've been worried sick about all the money he's been embezzling from Aunt Emily."

Whoa! Kyle had been embezzling money from Emily?

"What a dope I was. Scared senseless he'd wind up in jail, and all the while he and Ms. Nesbitt were planning to take the money and run off to the Cayman Islands."

So *that* was what Maggie had been worried about that day on the jogging track. Not that Kyle was a killer—but an embezzler. He and Nesbitt didn't need to kill Graham; they'd already stolen enough money for a new life in the Caymans. The only sins they'd been guilty of were embezzlement, adultery, and extremely tacky taste in sex games.

"I'm going to divorce that man so fast his head will spin," Maggie was ranting. "When I'm through with him, he won't be able to afford an olive for his martini."

Then she looked down and realized her glass was empty.

"Bartender!" she called out. "Another Cabocabana!"

But I barely heard her, a queasy feeling growing in the pit of my stomach.

I was convinced that whoever killed Graham had tried to kill me that afternoon. And there were only three people in the water who knew me: Kyle, Nesbitt, and Robbie.

If Kyle and Nesbitt were off the hook for Graham's murder, that left only one other person:

Robbie.

I knew from the get-go he was a bad boy. I just never dreamed he was this bad.

YOU'VE GOT MAIL

To: Jaineausten
From: DaddyO
Subject: Not My Fault!

I don't care what your mom says; I did *not* start that fire.

XXX,

Daddy

To: Jaineausten
From: Shoptillyoudrop
Subject: A Bit of Bad News

I hate to break this to you, sweetheart, when I know how much fun you must be having on your cruise, but I'm afraid Daddy has set fire to your apartment.

It's all because of his stupid pipe! Would you believe he emptied the dratted thing into the trash along with all the flammable rags from the paint and turpentine and walnut stain? It was only a matter of time before the bundle caught fire.

It must have been smoldering for hours. But we didn't notice it until we got back from a walk we took after dinner, where Daddy told me about some ridiculous plan to install beer keg faucets in your bathroom.

When we walked in the front door, the apartment was billowing with smoke. We raced to the kitchen and saw the trash can on fire and your kitchen curtains going up in flames.

Daddy tried to put out the fire with a bottle of Diet Coke, which, of course, didn't work, but luckily one of your neighbors smelled smoke and called the firemen, who came bursting through the front door and got everything under control in no time. No thanks to Daddy, I might add, who was hovering over them, giving them "pointers" on how to put out a fire! Honestly, I thought I'd die.

I'm happy to report that aside from your kitchen curtains nothing got destroyed. But I'm afraid your walls are covered with soot and have to be repainted. I called Ricardo, the handyman, and he's starting the job tomorrow. To think! If your father had only paid him that $30 in the beginning we wouldn't be paying an arm and a leg now!

But try not to fret, honey. Just remember you've got darling Lance waiting for you when you get back.

Love,

Mom

PS. The smoke in your apartment was so bad, we had to check into a hotel, a charming little place right across the street from the Century City shopping mall. I'll have to trot on over there to see what they have in the way of trousseau items, although I doubt they'll have anything as lovely as that pink sequined peignoir from the shopping channel. Did I mention it comes with a matching pink feather boa?

To: Jaineausten
From: DaddyO
Subject: Unjustly Accused!

I suppose your mom has written you all about the fire. Naturally, she blames me. She claimed the ashes from my pipe started it, but I'm not sure I sign off on that theory. I say those rags caught fire all by themselves in a burst of spontaneous combustion.

Needless to say, your mother panicked at the sight of the flames, but good old Daddy sprang to the rescue and put the fire out with some Diet Coke. Some idiot neighbor called the fire department, which was totally unnecessary. By the time the firemen showed up, I had everything well under control.

In spite of my heroism, I'm still in the doghouse with your mom. To keep peace in the family, I've agreed to let her hire that highway robber Ricardo to paint your apartment. Not only that, I made the supreme sacrifice and threw away my pipe. If that's not true love, I don't know what is.

Gotta run, lambchop. Your mom wants to go to the mall. And I can't afford to keep her waiting.

Hugs and kisses,

Daddy

PS. I know this is going to come as a blow, but I'm afraid I'm going to have to give up my plans to spruce up your apartment.

To: Jaineausten
From: Shoptillyoudrop
Subject: How Could You?

We just got back from the mall and found the most disturbing message from Lance. I can't believe you called off the wedding!!! How could you break Lance's heart like that—leaving him for a Cabo San Lucas cabana boy?

Your very disappointed,

Mom

PS. The only piece of good news I've had all day is that Daddy finally threw out that dratted pipe of his.

To: Jaineausten
From: DaddyO

Guess what? While your mom was running around shopping, I wandered into the most interesting store called Cigar-A-Rama. The sales clerk said I had the definite air of a cigar aficionado. I think he may be right. So I bought a few to try them out.

See you soon, sweetheart!

XXX

PS. What's all this about you being engaged to a cabana boy?

Chapter 21

What a fool I'd been to ignore Robbie as a suspect.

All his talk about being a laid-back surfer dude was just an act. The guy was undoubtedly just as moneygrubbing as Kyle and killed Graham to protect his inheritance.

I should have listened to my gut when I first met him. He was never really interested in me. He pursued me out of boredom, because there were no other women his age around. Then somehow he figured out I was investigating and got nervous. So he arranged for me to come along on the scuba excursion—not for the pleasure of my company, but to shut me up forever.

Talk about the Queen of Denial. Just because Robbie had a great tan and a seductive grin, I'd ruled him out as a potential killer.

But not anymore.

It was time to rein in my hormones and do something I should have done ages ago: break into his cabin and search for Graham's missing cuff links.

And so first thing the next morning I tracked down Samoa on his housekeeping rounds and threw myself on his mercy.

"Please, Samoa," I begged as he swabbed down a bathtub, "you've got to let me borrow that passkey."

He got up from the tub and clamped his arms resolutely across his chest.

"Samoa has two words for you, missy—Im Possible."

"I swear I'll bring it right back."

"Samoa no can do," he said, now swabbing the sink with gusto.

He sure as heck never cleaned my bathroom this well. I was lucky he brought me toilet paper.

"But it's a matter of life and death," I wailed, exaggerating just a tad.

"Samoa no can do," he repeated firmly.

I spent a few more minutes groveling, but he stuck with his "no can do" mantra.

What a pill. After all the editing I was doing for him, you'd think he'd let me have the stupid passkey.

Finally, I gave up and left him arranging towels on the towel rack. Which, I couldn't help noticing, were a damn sight fluffier than the car-wash rejects he brought me. I headed back out to the corridor and, in a moment of rebellion, swiped a couple of shampoos from his cart. That'd show him!

Oh, well. Who needed his silly passkey anyway? I'd just have to think of a way to break into Robbie's cabin without it.

But before I could break into Robbie's cabin, I still had one more class to teach.

I dreaded showing my face after the Nancy and

David Shaw fiasco, but I had no choice. I had a contract to honor. And we Austens always honor our commitments. Unless, of course, we can think of a really good excuse to get out of them.

I dragged myself over to the cavernous restaurant that served as my classroom.

All that was left of my original crew were Max, the napper; Amanda, the knitter; and Kenny, the *Scarlet Letter* scholar.

On the plus side, I was thrilled to see that Rita wasn't there.

At last, a ray of sunshine.

A ray that was quickly snuffed out when my wiry-haired nemesis came ambling in at the last minute with her two buddies—senoritas Marilyn and Judy.

"I brought my friends along," Rita informed me as she breezed past me with her gal pals in tow. "They had an hour to kill before Jazzercise."

"Actually, Rita, only enrolled students are permitted to take the class."

"You certainly have the space," she sneered, gesturing to the empty restaurant.

"Oh, all right," I sighed.

By now, I was a beaten woman. I'd given up all hope of teaching memoir writing to this bunch anyway. My only two eager students were long gone and, thanks to me, now on the brink of divorce.

With faint heart, I proceeded to hand out a series

of writing exercises. All of which were pretty much ignored as Amanda knitted, Rita gabbed with her posse, and Max caught up on his naps. On the plus side, I think Kenny got a lot of work done on his *Scarlet Letter* book report.

And to tell the truth, I wasn't exactly concentrating either.

All I could think about was that my shipboard romance, along with my apartment, had gone up in smoke. (Yes, once again I had been foolish enough to read my e-mails.)

I spent most of the hour (a) trying to figure out a way to break into Robbie's cabin and (b) kicking myself for not buying renter's insurance.

At last fifty-five minutes had crawled by and the class was drawing to a close.

"Any final questions?" I asked.

Kenny raised his hand. I perked up. Was it possible that my class had inspired the lad in some small way?

"Yes, Kenny?"

"I wanna know, does *Scarlet* have one *t* or two?"

So much for inspiration.

"One *t*," I sighed.

"How about 'letter'?" my budding scholar wanted to know.

Did these kids learn *nothing* in school?

I checked my watch and saw that it was time to put an end to my misery.

"Well, everyone, it looks like our time is up. I

want to thank you all for participating in our little workshop. I hope it's just the beginning of your adventures in the wonderful world of writing. Now would somebody please wake Max up?"

Kenny nudged Max awake, and the two of them filed out of class together.

"Cool class," I heard Kenny saying on his way out. "Especially the fight the other day. I shot a video of it on my cell phone. When I get home, I'm gonna put it on YouTube."

Oh, great. Just what the Shaws needed. A worldwide audience for their breakup.

Then, much to my surprise, Rita approached with her posse.

"Would you mind signing this?" she said, handing me a paper cocktail napkin.

"You want my autograph?" I asked, stunned.

Maybe I'd won her over after all. Maybe somehow I'd managed to gain her respect.

"In case you ever get famous," she said, exchanging smirks with her buddies. "It might be worth something on eBay."

I smiled stiffly and scribbled out my name on the napkin, leaving out the *i* in Jaine.

If I did get famous someday, I'd be damned if she'd make a penny.

By now, only Amanda was left in the class, still busy knitting.

"The class is over, Amanda," I called out to her.

"Just one minute, honey. I'm almost through." With that, she took out a pair of tiny scissors and snipped off the yarn, completing her handiwork.

Then she gathered her things together and walked over to me.

"I want to tell you how much I enjoyed your delightful class," she said. "Especially that interesting play we saw last week. About the couple getting a divorce. So very lifelike!"

"I'm glad you enjoyed it, Amanda."

"And as a token of my appreciation I hope you'll accept this little present."

With that, she handed me what she'd been knitting: a bright red pot holder.

"You made this for me?"

"You can use it around the campfire on your Arctic explorations," she nodded.

"Oh, Amanda!" I said, wrapping her in a hug. "This is the nicest thing that's happened to me on the whole darn cruise."

And it was. So what if the woman's porch light was a little dim? She was the one passenger on this ship who appreciated me!

I watched her walk away and came *thisclose* to crying. But I had to pull myself together. We part-time semi-professional P.I.s do not bust out crying over hand-knit pot holders.

So without any further ado, I blinked back my tears, squared my shoulders, and set out to trap a killer.

• • •

I'd come up with a plan. Somehow I'd get Robbie to invite me to his cabin, and once we were there, I'd miraculously think of a way to get rid of him and search for the cuff links. True, I hadn't worked out all the details. But it was better than nothing.

Unfortunately, my plan got off to a dismal start. I scoured the ship from stem to stern, but there was no sign of Robbie anywhere.

Finally, I gave up and sought solace at the buffet.

And that's when my luck turned. Just as I was scarfing down a most delicious ham and cheese panini, I glanced up and saw Robbie hurrying toward me.

"Jaine! I've been looking all over for you!"

"Mmfff," I said, my mouth full of panini.

"Ms. Nesbitt told me I'd probably find you in the buffet stuffing your face."

Okay, so he didn't say the part about me stuffing my face, but you can bet your bottom Pop-Tart that Nesbitt did.

"I've been so worried about you," he said, sitting across from me. "Are you okay?"

He looked at me with such concern, for a minute I wondered if I was wrong about him. Maybe he was nowhere near me in the water. Maybe Miguel was right. Maybe I did cut my hose on a rock.

Then again, maybe he was just a damn good actor.

"I'm fine," I said. "I'm afraid I overreacted yesterday."

"It's all my fault. I should've never let you out of my sight."

"It's okay. Really."

"Are you sure? Is there anything I can do for you? Anything at all?"

Time to launch Phase I of my plan.

"Now that you ask, I wouldn't mind some company this afternoon. I guess I am a bit shaken."

"Of course you are. And I insist on hanging out together."

He hit me with one of his lopsided grins, but for once, my heart did not go into meltdown mode.

"So what do you feel like doing?" he asked.

"Hey, I know!" I said as if I'd just thought of it. "How about a game of Scrabble?"

"Sure! Scrabble sounds great."

"Okay," I said, faking a smile. "Let's do it!"

"This should be fun," he said, as we got up to go. "But I've got to warn you. I'm a killer player."

That's exactly what I was afraid of.

We made our way over to the game room, looking like just another happy couple on vacation. Hah. If people only knew.

"Here we go," Robbie said, reaching for a Scrabble set.

I thought back to just a few nights ago when we were here in this same room hiding out from Anton. All I wanted then was to be alone with him, to have him take me in his arms and kiss me.

Now my palms were clammy at the thought of being stranded with him in his cabin.

"You want to play out by the pool?" he asked.

"It's so noisy out there," I said, trying to sound casual. "Why don't we go up to your cabin?"

"Um, sure."

He blinked, surprised. I could tell he was taken aback. Maybe he thought I was using Scrabble as an excuse to get frisky. Best to nip that thought in the bud.

"We can play out on your verandah," I said. "You do have one, don't you?"

"Yes, sure."

I figured he would, being up on the big-bucks deck.

"Wonderful! My cabin doesn't even have a window, and I'd love to spend at least one afternoon on a private verandah before the cruise is over."

"One private verandah coming right up!"

"Terrific," I said, as we took off for his cabin.

Phase I of my plan had been a success.

Now all I needed was a Phase II.

Chapter 22

It was another glorious day at sea, the sun glinting off the water, a gentle breeze wafting through the air.

Out on Robbie's verandah, I gazed over at my murder suspect, who was busy turning Scrabble tiles blank side up, his sun-bleached hair flopping onto his forehead, his knees knobby in cutoff jeans. And once more, I began having doubts.

Try as I might, it was hard to picture him as a cold-blooded killer. That caring look in his eyes when he saw me at the buffet seemed so genuine. Was he really that good an actor?

For a fleeting instant I was tempted to abandon my plan and just enjoy the afternoon playing Scrabble. But no, I had to hang tough. I couldn't let a pair of floppy bangs and knobby knees stand in the way of my investigation. I had to find out once and for all if Robbie was guilty.

The question was: How?

"Jaine? You ready to play?"

Robbie's tiles were already lined up on his rack.

And then it came to me. I knew what to do.

"Gee, Robbie," I said, with an apologetic smile, "I've changed my mind. I'm not really in the mood for Scrabble after all."

"Oh?" He looked up, surprised.

"I'd much rather play gin rummy. Would you

mind awfully going back to the game room and getting a deck of cards?"

"Okay. Sure."

I could tell he thought I was a bit of a ditz, but it couldn't be helped.

"I'll be right back," he said, heading into the cabin.

The minute I heard the door slam, I jumped up and dashed inside, making a beeline for the safe in his closet.

Okay, this was it. My golden opportunity. All I had to do was punch in the override code—

Omigosh. The override code! What the heck was it?? It had totally slipped my mind! How could I have been so stupid not to bring it with me? I wracked my brain trying to think of the mnemonic device I'd come up with to help me remember it.

Did an 89-year-old man marry a 36-year-old woman and have 2 children?

Frantically I punched in 89362.

No luck. Maybe a 36-year-old married an 82-year-old and had 9 children. No, that didn't work either. Okay, maybe a 28-year-old married a 93-year-old and had—

"Jaine! What are you doing?"

Oh, God. It was Robbie.

I whirled around and saw him standing behind me. I'd been so engrossed in my silly mnemonic device, I hadn't heard him come in.

"What are you doing back so soon?" I sputtered.

"When I got to the elevator, I realized I had a deck of cards in my desk drawer. But that's beside the point. The question is: what are you doing at my safe?"

By now his eyes had turned icy cold.

How on earth was I going to get out of this? What could I possibly say? *Just trying to convict you of murder?*

"I was . . . um . . . I was looking for the bathroom," I said, skittering past him, praying he wouldn't whip out a hidden ice pick.

"The bathroom is over there," he said, pointing clear across the room.

"No wonder I couldn't find it. I've got such a terrible sense of direction. Honest. I can't even figure out where I am in the YOU ARE HERE signs."

But Robbie wasn't interested in my fictional lack of navigation skills.

"I think you'd better go now," he said.

"Yeah, I guess I should. Hope I can find my way to the elevator, ha-ha."

I smiled feebly.

A smile that, needless to say, was not returned.

Something told me I'd seen the last of his lopsided grins.

I slinked off in disgrace, kicking myself for messing things up so badly. For crying out loud, even Prozac could have done a better job.

Trudging down the corridor to my cabin, I glanced up and saw that the door to Cookie's cabin was open. I peeked inside, and there she was, laying out some clothing on her bed.

Omigosh, they'd let her go! The captain must've found the real killer. In spite of my botched investigation, Cookie was a free woman!

"Cookie!" I cried as I raced to her side. "They've let you go."

"Not exactly," she replied, nodding to a fireplug of a security guy who'd squeezed himself into her tiny armchair. "They're just letting me pack my things before we dock tomorrow."

Then she reached into her closet and took down a suitcase.

"Oh." My heart sank.

"Tony," Cookie said to the fireplug as she plopped the suitcase on her bed, "give us a minute or two alone, okay?"

"I dunno," he said, his brow furrowed in what I was certain was unaccustomed thought. "The captain said I should stay with you."

"Give me a break, Tony. What do you think she's going to do—help me tunnel my way to freedom?"

"Oh, okay." He reluctantly pried himself from the chair. "But I'll be right outside."

The minute he lumbered off, Cookie turned to me eagerly.

"Well? Did you have any luck? Did you find out who really killed Graham?"

"I'm afraid not," I said, feeling about as clever as Tony.

"Oh."

"I have my eye on someone but I have no proof."

She forced a smile. "Oh, well. At least you tried."

I stood by helplessly as she started tossing clothes into her suitcase.

"I hope it hasn't been too awful for you in the brig."

"It's not so bad. The pillows are no lumpier than the ones here on the Paradise Deck. But I suppose it's the Taj Mahal compared to what it's going to be like in jail."

"I feel so responsible for all this," I sighed. "If only I'd done a better job, you wouldn't be in this predicament."

"Are you kidding?" She looked up from her packing. "You tried to help. I was the one crazy enough to get involved with Graham.

"When I think of all the years I wasted on that bum," she said, hurling a handful of underwear into the suitcase. "Never seeing through his lies, loaning him money for his silk shirts and his Botox shots and his Italian loafers. What an idiot I was."

Join the club, I felt like telling her, thinking of what a sap I'd been to fall for Robbie.

"Look, Cookie," I said, picking up a pair of panty hose that had fallen on the carpet, "I promise

I won't give up when we get to L.A. I'll keep on investigating until I find the killer."

I smiled bravely but it was all a front. I'd pretty much given up hope.

If Robbie knew I suspected him of murder, he was probably tossing those cuff links in the Pacific at this very minute.

Chapter 23

I spent the rest of the afternoon holed up in my cabin hacking away at Samoa's manuscript.

With an iron will, and a couple of Tylenol, I managed to make it through the chapter where our intrepid hero, ship's-steward-cum-secret-agent Samoa Huffington III (son of a colorful native hula dancer and a British earl), disarms a nuclear bomb with a toilet bowl plunger from his steward's cart.

See? All along I told you this stuff was beyond belief, and you scoffed. You thought to yourself, she's got to be exaggerating. Now you know.

By the time Secret Agent 12 ½ (which also happened to be the size of his ginormous private part) had saved the world from nuclear destruction, it was time for dinner.

I knew this because Prozac had been clawing my thighs for the past half hour.

Once more, I steered clear of the dining room and brought back chow from the buffet—baby back ribs and mashed potatoes for me, and Chilean sea bass for Prozac.

It was all very delicious. Things taste so much better, I find, when you're not sitting at a table full of murder suspects.

After dinner, I took a quick shower and changed into my jammies, then hunkered down to tackle the final fifty pages of *Do Not Distub*, wherein Secret Agent 12 ½ decimates a vicious band of international terrorists with a bottle of Windex.

At last I'd finished. Samoa Huffington III had driven off into the sunset in his Samoamobile with his true love, a buxom nuclear physicist named Passionata Von Cleef.

With Herculean effort I'd slogged my way through nine hundred pages of the most nauseating goop to come down the pike since the Valdez oil spill.

I decided to celebrate with one final brownie run at the buffet.

Too lazy to get dressed, I threw a raincoat over my PJs. Ten minutes later I was back, bearing brownies and shrimp.

"Look what Mommy brought, Pro! Yummy shri—"

But I was talking to thin air. Prozac was nowhere in sight.

I knew she wasn't hiding because Prozac never plays hard to get when it comes to snacks. I checked out the bathroom, hoping I would find her kicking sand around in her litter box. But she wasn't there either.

And then I noticed that Samoa had been in to turn down the beds. Dammit. He must've left the door open again. For crying out loud, he knew there was a cat in my cabin. Couldn't he remember to shut a simple door?

Sure enough, I saw a note from him propped up on my night table:

Cat mising. Sneke out when I com to tun down bed. Your very sinserly, Samoa

Disgusted, I crumpled the note and hurled it across the room, then dashed out into the corridor. I spotted Prozac right away, a few cabins down, inhaling leftovers from a room service tray.

I raced over to her, but when she saw me coming, she took off like a shot. I watched in horror as she headed for the elevators.

Oh, Lord, I prayed, *please don't let her get on an elevator full of people.*

My prayers were answered. Sort of. She didn't get on an elevator. Instead she sprinted up a flight of stairs just opposite the elevators, her tail swishing with glee. She was loving every minute of this.

I huffed up the stairs, my coat flapping open behind me, racing past an elderly couple who stared openmouthed at my rubber duckie pajamas.

(Did I not mention my pajamas had rubber duckies on them? Well, they did. They were a Shopping Channel gift from my mom, who sometimes labors under the illusion that I am still a fifth grader.)

"Pajama party on the Aloha Deck!" I cried, then resumed chasing Prozac, who had abandoned the stairs and was now charging down a corridor.

I was delighted to see her run into an alcove.

The little devil was trapped!

Or so I thought.

When I got there I saw an open door in the alcove. And Prozac's tail disappearing behind it.

I followed her into what was clearly the crew's passageway.

Gone were the carpets and fancy wallpaper. Here, it was linoleum flooring and pea-green paint on the walls.

Prozac, having been cooped up in a cell-like cabin for the past six days, was not about to be taken back into captivity. She sprinted down the corridor in a joyous game of Catch Me If You Can, leading me and my pounding heart into a stairwell up several more flights and then down a byzantine maze of corridors.

I ran after her as fast as I could, garnering more than a few slack-jawed reactions from passing crew members.

Some of them tried to catch Prozac, but she evaded them all with impressive skill.

Others tried to stop me.

I had no choice but to lob them with the shrimp I'd hurriedly shoved in my raincoat pocket as I'd dashed out of my cabin. Which turned out to be quite effective. Nothing quite stops a person in his tracks like a flying shrimp.

At one point, a burly maintenance man jutted in front of me and blocked my path.

"No passengers allowed in crew quarters," he scolded.

By now I'd used up all my shrimp, so I was forced to pelt him with one of the brownies I'd shoved in my other pocket.

Man, I hated to lose that brownie. But on the plus side, I managed to slip past him as he wiped chocolate frosting off his nose.

Seconds later he was back tugging at my coat sleeve, but I wriggled out of the coat and charged ahead. It was amazing, really, how fast I was running. As you well know from my little episode on the jogging track, I was not exactly in tip-top aerobic condition. But I guess I was like the ninety-nine-pound woman who lifts a car to save her child. Somewhere inside me I summoned the speed to evade my would-be captors.

Unfortunately, though, my encounter with the maintenance man had slowed me down. By the time I broke away from him, I'd lost sight of Prozac.

I kept running anyway, hoping I'd catch up with

her. And then suddenly the corridor came to a dead end. I stood facing a large, dark, curtained-off area. Probably some sort of storage facility. In the middle was a table with black cloth draped over it.

And there—thank heavens—leaping onto the table was Prozac!

I brushed past a shadowy figure in black and dashed over to where Prozac was now busy licking her privates.

She looked up at me and yawned.

My, that was fun!

So happy was I to finally see her that I refrained from giving her the stern shriekfest she so richly deserved.

Instead, I scooped her up in my arms.

And just as I did I heard a deep voice booming from above:

"And now, ladies and gentlemen, the one, the only—The Great Branzini!"

I looked around and suddenly became aware of ropes and cables and overhead klieg lights.

Holy Mackerel. This little cul de sac I'd wandered onto wasn't a storage area—but a stage! And that shadowy figure in black was The Great Branzini!

I was in the Grand Showroom!

Before I knew it, the curtains were parting and there I was in my rubber duckie pajamas, clutching Prozac in front of three hundred astonished passengers.

Prozac blinked out at the audience.

Anybody out there got tuna?

Minutes later two beefy security guards were escorting me and Prozac to Captain Lindstrom's office.

Needless to say, the good captain was none too pleased to see us.

"You smuggled a cat on board ship?" he cried, aghast at the sight of Prozac in my arms.

"Well, technically, she smuggled herself on board; by the time I found out, it was too late to do anything about it."

"You smuggled a cat on board ship," he repeated, ignoring my argument for the defense.

Then he proceeded to launch into a recap of my many sins.

"You're responsible for two of our passengers getting a divorce. You tried to cheat another passenger out of first prize at Musical Men. You were caught stealing sand from our sandbox. And now you show up on stage in the Grand Showroom in those ridiculous chicken pajamas!"

"Actually, they're not chickens," I pointed out. "They're rubber duckies."

Once again, he chose to ignore the technical side of things and continued ranting about my many shortcomings as a lecturer, a passenger, and a pet owner.

It's all too painful to repeat in detail, but the gist

of it was that I was persona non grata on Holiday—and probably every other cruise line on the planet.

Finally, the good captain ran out of steam and glanced down at Prozac in my arms, who was purring like a buzz saw. She had no idea what hot water she was in.

"So what's her name?" he asked.

"Prozac."

"Very appropriate, considering her owner."

Then he added, in a somewhat more mellow tone of voice, "She is a cute little thing, isn't she?"

Prozac, sensing she was being talked about, launched into her Adorable Act: big green eyes, tilted head, tail wagging saucily.

The sap fell for it like a ton of bricks.

"Come here, sweetheart."

He plucked her from my arms and plopped her into his ample lap.

Prozac, the shameless hussy, rubbed against his belly with wild abandon.

"It's never the fault of the animal," Captain Lindstrom cooed into her ear. "It's always the owner."

She looked up at him with her baby greens.

Yes, she is impossible, isn't she?

"Maybe we don't have to put you in quarantine," he said, scratching behind her ears. "After all, it's just for one night. How would you like to stay with me, in the captain's suite?"

By now she was rubbing against him with such fervor, I feared she'd soon be giving birth to Scandinavian kittens.

"You wait here while I get her settled," he snapped at me, "and I'll be back with a release form for you to sign.

"Come on, Strudel Face," he cooed to Prozac.

Strudel Face?? And this man was in charge of a one-hundred-sixteen-ton ship??

"Let's go set you up in Uncle Karl's suite. You hungry, darling? How would you like a nice filet mignon from the kitchen?"

She purred in ecstasy.

Extra rare, please.

Oh, for crying out loud. I'd been dying for a steak all week, and now Prozac was the one getting it!

Then he carried her out, murmuring a most nauseating stream of baby talk.

If I'd known she'd be fawned over like this, I would've turned her in days ago. All that sneaking and worrying and delivering her meals—not to mention editing Samoa's god-awful manuscript!

Oh, well. On the plus side, at least I could sleep with a pillow tonight.

I sat back to wait for Lindstrom to return with my release form. He sure was taking his time. Probably busy giving Prozac a massage.

After a while, I got up and started nosing around,

thumbing through Lindstrom's date book and checking out his screensaver (the sinking of the *Titanic*, in case you're interested). I even peeked into his private bathroom.

And after the cavalier way he treated me, I have no compunctions whatsoever about blabbing to the world that Captain Karl Lindstrom of Holiday Cruise Lines is the proud owner of Volumes I–VII of *Jokes for the John*.

Finally, I wandered over to gaze at the historical photos on the walls. My eyes lingered on the picture of Emily, the one taken so long ago, when she was just a girl. She was so young, so hopeful, in her shirtwaist dress and penny loafers and locket around her neck—

Wait a minute. Now that I looked closely, I saw it wasn't a locket.

I squinted to get a better look.

Holy Moses. It was a half a heart!

Just like the half a heart Graham gave Cookie and dozens of other women over the years.

But he couldn't possibly have given that one to Emily. When that picture was taken, Graham was just a child.

Or was he? Just this afternoon Cookie said that she'd loaned Graham money for Botox shots. What if Graham had been a lot older than he looked? Was it possible Graham was Emily's first love, the one who'd broken her heart? Robbie told me her lover was a member of the ship's crew. And yesterday at lunch Kyle said Graham had been a steward all his life.

And hadn't Robbie also said that her lover had accepted a bribe from Emily's father to disappear from her life? Was Graham the one who'd accepted that bribe and deserted her all those years ago?

No doubt, he forgot her as soon as the next cruise set sail. But maybe Emily never forgot. Maybe she'd been harboring a resentment all these years. And then they met again. She'd changed so much since that long-ago picture, Graham probably didn't recognize her. But she recognized him. Women rarely forget a first love, especially one who's been Botoxed into perennial youth.

All the old hurt and pain must have come flooding back. Her life had been lonely and unfulfilled. And here he was, still handing out the same phony love tokens to unsuspecting women.

It was all too much for her.

So she decided to seek revenge with a stolen ice pick.

Oh, Lord. It all made sense.

I was staring into space, dumbstruck, when Captain Lindstrom finally returned with the release form.

I signed it in a daze.

"You can pick up your cat when we dock

tomorrow," he said. "Do you think you can manage to stay out of trouble until then?"

The answer, as it turned out, was a resounding No.

Chapter 24

I stumbled out of Lindstrom's office in a daze. Sweet Aunt Emily—a killer? I had been wrong so often in this case; was I making yet another mistake?

There was only one way to find out. Somehow I had to break into Emily's cabin and search for Graham's missing cuff links. After my recent fiasco with Robbie, I dreaded the thought, but I had no other choice.

And then I remembered that Emily was being sedated every night. If she was in a deep enough sleep, I'd be able to snoop around without waking her. The trouble was—how to get rid of Ms. Nesbitt? Robbie told me she'd been spending the night with Emily, sleeping on her sofa.

The answer came to me in a flash. I'd dangle a carrot in front of her. A carrot named Kyle.

I hurried back to my cabin, garnering my fair share of boggled looks. You'd think no one had ever seen a pair of rubber duckie pajamas in an elevator before.

After a quick change of clothes, I made my way

to Emily's suite, praying she'd already been sedated.

Nesbitt came to the door in a flannel bathrobe and granny nightgown, her horn-rimmed glasses perched on her nose. Quite a difference from the Hubba Hottie outfit she'd worn for her sexcapade with Kyle.

"Yes?" she snapped, ever the charmer.

"I'm sorry to bother you, Leona, but I just ran into Kyle, and he said he needs to talk to you."

"Then why didn't he call?" she asked, peering at me over her glasses.

Oops. Hadn't thought of that.

"Um . . . he was afraid of waking Emily."

"Oh, she's dead to the world."

Good news indeed.

"Anyhow," I said, "Kyle's waiting for you in the Tiki Lounge. He must be worried about one of Emily's investments. He said something about trouble with a bank account in the Cayman Islands."

Her lips clamped shut in a thin, angry line. I could practically hear her thinking, *There goes the love nest.*

"Look, do you mind watching Emily for a while?"

"Be happy to." I forced a genial smile.

"Great." She volleyed my phony smile right back at me and dashed off to get dressed for her nonexistent rendezvous.

I headed into the sitting area of the suite and saw

the indentations on the sofa where Nesbitt had been lying, a romance novel she'd been reading splayed open on the coffee table.

Then I slipped through the archway to Emily's bedroom, where I was reassured to find her lying on her back sleeping soundly, her chest moving up and down in regular intervals. In the light from the sitting area, I could see her parchment skin cross-hatched with wrinkles, her thinning silver hair forming a lacy nimbus on her pillow.

She looked so sweet, so frail. Would she even have had the strength to go after Graham with an ice pick?

Time to find out.

I hurried to the safe in her walk-in closet. This time you'll be glad to know I remembered to bring the override code.

I punched in the numbers and cringed at the sound of the beeps. In the tomblike quiet of the cabin, they sounded like cannons. I peeked out into the bedroom and sighed with relief to see Emily still out like a light. I had to stop being such a nervous Nelly. The woman was on serious sleep meds. She wasn't about to wake up.

I returned to the safe and took a deep breath.

With trembling hands, I opened it.

The light in the closet was dim, but I was able to make out what was inside: A string of pearls. Matching earrings. A cameo broach. Passport and wallet.

But no cuff links.

Oh, well. It was possible she stashed them some-where else in the cabin, so I started snooping around.

At one point, as I was pulling open the door to one of her bedside night tables, she stirred in her sleep. My heart began racing. What on earth could I possibly say if she woke up?

But thank heavens, she just rolled over on her side and continued breathing deeply.

I searched the suite as thoroughly as I dared, but there was no sign of the cuff links. Finally, I threw in the towel and admitted defeat.

I was just about to slink off into the night when I passed the coffee table in the sitting area. There in the center of the table was the bowl of wax fruit I almost bit into the night of Emily's cocktail party.

How strange, now that I thought about it. Most people don't tote along a bowl of wax fruit on their travels.

And then it hit me. What if it was some sort of security device, like those phony rocks people use to hide their keys? Emily might not want to trust her valuables to a rinky-dink safe that an amateur like me could break into.

One by one I checked out the pieces of fruit, shaking them to see if they were hollow.

But they were all just what they seemed to be: wax fruit.

Then I reached the final pear at the bottom of the bowl.

I picked it up and felt a frisson of excitement when I realized it was lighter than the others.

I shook it and heard rattling inside.

When I held it under a lamp on the end table, I was able to discern a faint line running around the circumference, dividing the pear in half.

I could feel my heart pounding as I twisted the two halves apart.

Then I said a little prayer and peered inside.

Bingo. There they were: Graham's diamond cuff links.

At last I knew who the killer was. And I had the evidence to prove it.

I was tempted to take the cuff links with me, but that would be tampering with state's evidence—a bit of a no-no in legal circles. So I reluctantly left them behind and set out to find Captain Lindstrom. Somehow I had to convince him to conduct an official search of Emily's cabin.

By now I knew the way to his office, but I doubted he'd still be there, not at this time of night. My guess was he was tucked away in his suite giving Prozac a belly rub.

I hurried to the lobby reception desk.

"I need to talk to the captain," I said to one of the clerks on duty, a cool blond Paige wannabe.

"I'm afraid he's not available right now," Ms.

Wannabe replied, with a plastic smile. "May I be of assistance?"

"No, you may not. Just take me to the captain."

"That's impossible," she said, her smile still firmly in place "He's busy steering the ship and cannot be disturbed."

How frustrating! What the heck was he doing steering the ship, anyway? Didn't he have first mates and bo'suns and ship steerers for stuff like that?

I would've broken the rules and busted in on him but I had no idea where this ship-steering action took place. And Ms. Wannabe was not about to tell me. I made her promise to have the captain contact me the minute he was through, and I started back to my cabin.

But then I had the bad luck to bump into Ms. Nesbitt.

"What's going on?" she scowled. "Kyle's not in the Tiki Lounge."

I put on my most innocent face.

"I swear, Leona, he was there just a little while ago."

She shot me a look that could wilt steel. "And why aren't you with Emily?"

"Um . . . she woke up and asked me to get her a magazine. I'm on my way to buy it now."

Nesbitt snorted in disbelief.

"That's impossible! I gave her two sleeping pills. How could she wake up?"

"Beats me," I shrugged, and scooted off before she could continue her inquisition.

Back in my cabin, I stretched out on my bed, waiting for the captain's call. This time, I could not possibly allow him to blow me off.

I was in the middle of rehearsing a very stern speech, threatening to sue Holiday Cruise Lines all the way up to the Supreme Court if need be, when I heard a knock on the door.

"Who is it?"

"Message from the captain," a woman, probably Ms. Wannabe, replied.

But it wasn't Ms. Wannabe. Which I should have figured out at the time. If I'd had half a brain cell working, I would have recognized whose voice it really was. But so eager was I to speak with the captain, I raced to the door and flung it open. Only to find Emily standing there in a sweat suit, her normally mild blue eyes blazing.

In her hand she clutched one of Anton's ice picks.

I was so caught off guard at the sight of her that I was an easy target when she shoved me back into my cabin. What happened to the frail old lady I'd seen lying in bed just a little while ago? The fiery little dynamo who'd just given me a shove had definitely been eating her Wheaties.

As she lunged at me, I made a mad dash for the bathroom, slithering in just before the ice pick came crashing down on the door frame. Frantically I locked the door and began screaming for help. Surely someone was bound to hear me.

If only I had a phone in the bathroom! But this was the Dungeon Deck. I was lucky I had hot and cold running water.

So busy was I screaming bloody murder that I didn't hear Emily jimmying the bathroom lock with the ice pick. By the time I did hear it, it was too late. Suddenly there she was, charging in the door.

All I could think of was the shower scene in *Psycho*. Oh, Lord! I was going to wind up dead in the bathroom like poor Janet Leigh!

I looked around, frantic, for something to defend myself with and grabbed the first thing I saw—Prozac's litter box.

I flung the contents in Emily's face and felt a surge of joy when she was temporarily blinded. My joy was short-lived, however. Because when I raced past her to what I thought was freedom, I slipped on the sand. I tried to regain my balance but stumbled out into the bedroom and fell flat on my face. By the time I sat up, Emily was standing over me clutching her trusty ice pick.

"What on earth are you doing with a litter box in your bathroom?" she sputtered, spitting sand from her mouth.

"It's for my cat. She's a stowaway."

"Really, Jaine," she tsked. "A stowaway? How

very foolish. But then, you're a very foolish girl, aren't you?"

"I suppose so." I had to keep her talking and pray that someone had heard me screaming.

"So," I said, "I guess you weren't really sleeping when I was in your cabin just now."

"Of course not, dear," she said, flicking a piece of cat poop from her shoulder. "I never take those silly pills Leona gives me. I don't need sedatives. I've been happy as a clam ever since I killed Graham. But I played the role of the grieving fiancée quite beautifully, didn't I?"

"Oh, very," I said, inching away from her on my tush. "You had us all convinced you really loved him."

"I did, so very much when I was young and naive. But Graham was an evil man. He pretended he loved me and wanted to marry me. But when Daddy offered him money to leave me, he didn't hesitate to take it. He was gone like a shot. He broke my heart."

For a brief flicker, her eyes turned vulnerable. But they quickly hardened again.

"And then, all these years later, when he saw me on the ship, he didn't even remember me. I thought about him every day of my life, and he didn't even know who I was. He was still playing his same old games, giving out those sentimental pendants to foolish women.

"Evil like that must be punished," she said, a

mad gleam in her eyes. "It says so in the Bible."

Holy Mackerel. Emily clearly had more than a few screws loose.

"The minute I saw those ice picks, I knew how Graham would meet his end. It was just a matter of when. And then, after Cookie made that big scene in the Grand Showroom, I knew the time had come. If anything happened to Graham, everyone would blame her.

"I followed Graham after he dropped me off at my cabin that night, hiding in the shadows as he met with Cookie and told her he was just waiting for me to die and inherit my money.

"Such a dreadful man," she tsked. "Such a pleasure to stab him in the heart. A fitting end, don't you think, after all the hearts he'd broken?"

"Absolutely!" I said. "In fact, the more I think about it, the more I'm convinced you did the right thing. So why don't you just put away that ice pick, and it'll be our little secret?"

I flashed her what I hoped was a trustworthy smile.

"Nice try, dear. But it won't work. As we say at sea, you're dead in the water. It's all your own fault, you know. You really should have minded your own business."

She wagged the ice pick at me reprovingly.

"I suspected something was up when Ms. Nesbitt told me you'd been questioning her. And then when I heard you on your cell phone in Cabo, talking about your plan to go to the police, I simply had to stop you. I tried to scare you off by cutting your scuba hose."

"You?" I blinked in surprise. "But you weren't even in the water."

"Of course not, dear. I hired one of the busboys in the restaurant to do it for me. Remember when I broke down and ran to the ladies' room in tears? Well, those tears were just an act. Part of my performance. And I wasn't in the ladies' room. I was outside the men's room paying a darling busboy named Jaime two hundred dollars to snip your air hose. I told him that it was a practical joke. That you were an experienced scuba diver. I don't think he really believed me, but for two hundred dollars, he was happy to oblige. Labor is so reasonable in Mexico, don't you think?"

So Nesbitt had been right. It *was* one of the locals!

"But did you take the hint? Noooo. You went right on snooping and spying, and now it's come to this."

By now I'd inched my way up against the wall, not easy to do from a sitting position. Unfortunately, Emily had inched her way right along with me.

"Well, this is it, Jaine. Time to go to that great cruise ship in the sky."

She tested the tip of her ice pick and smiled.

"Nice and sharp."

Was it really going to end like this? Hacked to death by a crazy lady in a poop-stained sweat suit? I was too young to die! I hadn't been to Paris. Or Rome. Or the Ben & Jerry factory tour in Waterbury, Vermont!

What the heck was wrong with me? I couldn't just sit there, cringing like a coward, and let her kill me without putting up a fight.

I had to do something. Now!

And so, as she knelt down to get better aim at me, I kicked her in the shins with every ounce of strength I had. Which, from my awkward position on the floor, wasn't much. But it was enough to send her stumbling backward.

Free at last from her hovering ice pick, I leapt to my feet and charged at her.

You'd think I'd have an easy time of it. After all, she was at least three decades older than me. But the woman had the strength of the truly insane. Not to mention that darn ice pick clutched in her hand.

Just as I was biting her wrist in an attempt to get her to drop it, she snuck in a blow to my stomach that sent me reeling.

The next thing I knew she had me straddled on the bed.

"Okay, Jaine," she said, her face grim with determination. "It's all over. No more games."

It looked like my time was up. The End. Finito.

But then, just as I was preparing to take my last

breath on the planet, I saw it: Samoa's manuscript, where I'd tossed it on my night table.

I waited till Emily raised the ice pick above her head to gain thrust, and in that millisecond while her arms were raised, I grabbed the manuscript and held it over my chest.

She plunged the pick with the force of an Olympian. But it barely made a dent in the massive tome.

Furious, she raised the pick to give it another shot, but she never got a chance. Because just then two security guards came rushing into the room.

Thank heavens someone must have heard my screams and called for help.

There was much scuffling and shouting as they pried her off me and wrenched the ice pick from her hands.

But I barely registered what was happening.

All I could think of was that my life had been saved by *Do Not Distub*!

Minutes later Captain Lindstrom showed up and at last listened to what I had to say. He quickly dispatched minions to search Emily's cabin.

Then he turned to the security guys, who had Emily by the elbows.

"Let her go," he commanded, holding out his arm to her in a courtly gesture.

"Shall we, Miss Pritchard?"

"Of course, captain," she said, smiling serenely.

"I'm afraid you're going to have to spend the night in custody."

"Oh, I don't mind. I've always wanted to see a ship's brig. How very exciting!"

Gone was the vengeful madwoman who'd just tried to eviscerate me with an ice pick, and in her place was the slightly eccentric old lady who'd greeted me so effusively that first night at sea.

"You mustn't worry about me, Karl," she said. "I don't regret what I did, not for a minute.

"The only thing I do regret," she added, with a sly smile in my direction, "was my bad luck in dinner companions."

And then she headed out the door on the captain's arm, her eyes as clear and bright as they'd been all those years ago on her very first cruise.

Chapter 25

Those of you keeping track of my calorie intake—I'm glad you are, because I'm not—know that I never did get to eat those brownies I'd brought back to my cabin ages ago.

And by now I was starving. Near-death experiences tend to make me a bit peckish.

So I zipped over to the buffet to make up for lost chocolate.

I'd just polished off my second brownie and was licking the frosting from my fingers when I looked up and saw Robbie making his way across the nearly deserted room.

I slumped down in my seat, dreading the thought of facing him. Not only had he caught me attempting to break into his safe, but now I was going to have to tell him his beloved Aunt Emily was a psychopathic killer.

"I figured I'd find you here," he said, sitting across from me.

"Look, Robbie, there's something I should tell you."

"If it's about Aunt Emily," he sighed, "I already know. The captain told us."

"I'm so sorry."

"To tell the truth, I'm not all that surprised."

"You aren't?"

"Aunt Em's always been slightly off-kilter. As she grew older, I sensed it more and more. That's why I was so happy when she hooked up with Graham. He seemed to be so good for her." He smiled ruefully. "Could I have been more wrong? I never dreamed he'd be the one to send her over the edge.

"But the strange thing is, when I went to see her just now, she didn't seem upset. It's as if killing Graham brought her peace somehow."

"I know just what you mean," I said, thinking of how calmly she'd walked off with Captain Lindstrom.

"We'll get her the best attorneys money can buy

and hope they get her off with an insanity plea. The poor defenseless thing doesn't belong in prison."

If you ask me, Emily was more than capable of defending herself in prison, but I kept my mouth shut.

"Anyhow, Jaine," he said, frowning, "I'm here because I want to talk about what happened today in my cabin."

I cringed at the memory.

"I'm so sorry about that, Robbie. I swear, I'm not a thief."

"I know you're not. You were looking for the cuff links."

"You knew that?"

He nodded. "I figured you suspected one of us of killing Graham. I was just so hurt that you thought it was me."

"Oh, but I didn't suspect you!"

He shot me a laser look.

"Okay, so maybe I did suspect you. But my heart wasn't in it. Honest! You do believe me, don't you?"

I waited for an agonizing beat.

And then—hallelujah!—his lopsided grin made a triumphant return.

"I believe you," he said. "And by the way, if you had looked in my safe, you would've found this."

He took a small jewelry box from his pocket and handed it to me.

"Go ahead. Open it."

I did and found a lovely silver dolphin pin inside. "It's beautiful!"

"One of these days," he grinned, "we're going to swim with the dolphins."

Okay, this was it. I had to come clean and tell him the only thing I wanted to go swimming with was a rubber float in a heated pool, preferably with a built-in holder for a gin and tonic.

But this was me we're talking about. So the words that actually came out of my mouth were: "I can't wait!"

Oh, well. I had to look on the bright side. Compared to the dolphins, I'd look positively anorexic.

Then he reached over and took my hand, and the same electric jolt I'd felt that night out on deck coursed through my body.

"Oh, no," he groaned, taking his hand back.

"What's wrong?"

"Don't look now, but that idiot ice sculptor is coming."

"But that's impossible."

Surely Anton wasn't still interested in me after our last encounter in my cabin.

How wrong I was. I turned and saw him trotting over to our table, ponytail swaying, holding a covered plate in his hand.

"Jaine, babe!" he leered, his libido alive and kicking. "I've been looking all over for you."

Apparently it no longer bothered him that I knew

all about his checkered past as the Butterfly Bandit.

"Look what I sculpted for you. An egg salad Kiss."

He whipped off the cover of the plate, and sure enough, there on the plate was a reasonably good facsimile of a Hershey's Kiss in egg salad.

"Whaddaya think? Terrific, huh?"

At which point, Robbie got up from the table and stood between us.

"Sorry, buddy," he said. "She's already got a kiss."

And right there, in the middle of the twenty-four-hour buffet, he took me in his arms and kissed me.

Needless to say, I went back for seconds.

YOU'VE GOT MAIL

To: Jaineausten
From: Hot-to-Trotsky
Subject: Wedding with Me

Hello, Ms. Jaine Austen—

My name Vladimir Ivan Trotsky. I come from beautiful land of Uzbekistan. I meet your beautiful mother at Universal Studios Tour and she tell me all about you, what a beautiful woman you are, what beautiful cook and homemaker.

I am tall, dark, and very beautiful, too. Plus I have all my own teeth. So I write to see if you be interested in wedding with me?

Write back and we will arrange dowry.

Yours very sincerely,

Vladimir Ivan Trotsky

Epilogue

Needless to say, I did not marry Vladimir Ivan Trotsky—in spite of his tempting offer to shower me with all the yogurt I could eat and a goat of my very own.

Back here in the States, Emily Pritchard is out on bail and awaiting her murder trial in a luxury sanitarium for the Rich & Cuckoo.

Her lawyers are confident they'll get her off on an insanity plea.

She was certainly sane enough to disinherit Kyle when Maggie spilled the beans about his embezzlement. To avoid a jail sentence, Kyle returned all the money he hadn't already spent. Needless to say, he and Nesbitt never made it to the Cayman Islands. Last I heard, they were foaming lattes at a Starbucks in Burbank.

Free from Kyle's tyranny, Maggie got a job as an assertiveness training counselor and is dating a guy she met at Gamblers Anonymous.

Cookie Esposito sued Holiday Cruise Lines for false arrest and settled out of court for a small fortune. She quit the cruise biz and settled down in Palm Springs, where she married a mega-wealthy widower. For their honeymoon, they sailed around the world on their own private yacht. The only time she sings now is in her travertine marble shower.

And speaking of happy couples, you'll never guess who kissed and made up on the flight back home to Seattle? That's right, Nancy and David—the battling Bickersons from my class. David wrote me a letter of apology for yelling at me at the pier in Puerto Vallarta. He said that, thanks to having aired their repressed resentments in my class, he and Nancy are now happier than ever.

(What's more, he's actually proud of the fact that Kenny's YouTube video of their fight has scored over two million hits.)

As for Irritating Rita? She really did try to sell my autographed cocktail napkin on eBay—and had the nerve to start the bidding at fifty cents! There was only one bidder, some sap who wound up paying three bucks. I should be getting it in the mail any day now.

On the home front, you'll be happy to know that Ricardo did a very nice job painting my apartment. True, my first choice in colors would not have been "Tropical Orange," but I've cleverly toned it down by wearing sunglasses indoors.

Lance is dating Jean-Paul, the baker he met while planning "our" wedding. I sure hope it lasts. The guy's éclairs are to die for.

For some insane reason, despite phone calls and e-mails to the contrary, Mom refuses to believe that Lance is really gay. According to her, it's just a phase. Having convinced herself that we're bound to eventually tie the knot, she went ahead and ordered me a wedding dress from The Shopping Channel. It's a genuine Vera Wang knockoff. Only $89.95 plus shipping and handling.

Of course, you're probably wondering whatever happened to my relationship with Robbie. Me, too. I haven't seen him since the cruise. It turns out that his little surfboard business isn't so little after all. It's what you (and *Fortune* magazine) might call one of California's most successful privately owned corporations.

One week after we got back from the cruise he took off to oversee the opening of his new San Diego offices and wound up staying there for three months. He finally got back last week and called me.

The good news is, I'm seeing him tomorrow. The bad news is, we're going snorkeling.

Well, gotta run. Her royal highness needs her back scratched.

Catch you next time.

PS. You're not going to believe this, but Samoa's book actually got published! According to the *New York Times Book Review*, *Do Not Distub* is "a classic example of absurdist literature at its most absurd." What's more, it's soon to be a major motion picture, starring Antonio Banderas as Samoa Huffington III.

Center Point Publishing
600 Brooks Road ● PO Box 1
Thorndike ME 04986-0001 USA

(207) 568-3717

US & Canada:
1 800 929-9108
www.centerpointlargeprint.com